BOUNTY OF ASH

THE PHOENIX SERIES - BOOK TWO

SARAH ROCKWOOD

QUEEN & KING ENTERTAINMENT

COME CLOSER

Come closer. The story doesn't end on the page.

Want early access to new releases, behind-the-scenes world building, and occasional letters from my strange and unusual world?

You'll also be the first to know when new episodes of my podcast, *We Make Art*, go live—conversations and reflections for creatives who want to live wide awake.

Sign up and join me on this adventure:

https://sarahrockwood.com/mailing-list/

1

———

The phone was ringing. I tried to ignore it, but it kept going. Sunlight burned through my eyelids, making a return to sleep impossible. I tumbled from my bed and made my way to the living room. I pawed at the phone until it came loose from its cradle and pressed it to my face, somewhere near my mouth.

"Hello," I croaked.

"Phoenix? Sweetie, are you okay? You sound sick!"

My entire body snapped to attention.

"No mom, I just woke up."

"It's 11 AM! You just got up?"

"Mother, don't start."

She would anyway.

"Don't speak to me like that, Phoenix."

"Mom, I'm sorry. I..."

I stopped cold. I could see myself in the mirror above the sofa. I had wings. Big, giant, multicoloured wings. On my sleepy march to the phone, I'd forgotten all about them.

"Whoa," I whispered.

I reached back to touch them, and there was nothing

there. Panicking, I looked over one shoulder and then the other like a slow-witted dog searching for its tail. There was nothing there. Nothing. No wings protruding from my back, no beautiful feathers framing me. They were only visible in my reflection. Crazy. And problematic. Going to the ladies' room would raise a few eyebrows.

"Phoenix? Are you listening to me?"

Right, my mother was still talking.

"Yes, mom. Sorry, mom. Could you repeat that?"

She sighed loudly.

"When can we expect you this afternoon?"

"This afternoon?"

I'd Travelled back to the exact moment in time I had left when I went on my wing finding adventure. Which made today was my brother's birthday. Crap. And there was a big family dinner. Double crap. I had to get out of this.

"Well, Mom, I'm not really feeling that well."

"Nonsense. You're fine." Her voice was like cold iron. My Mom definitely had some powers of her own. "You want to live a life of big city excess that's your choice, but I'll not have you taking that out on your brother."

She had slipped into her 'big city evils' routine. Although I highly doubted my brother would miss my appearance at his, quote-en-quote, party, Mom was gearing up for an epic rant, and there was only one way to defuse this ticking time bomb.

"I'll be there at 6."

"You'll be here at 5."

"Yes, mother."

"Love you, sweetie."

She hung up. I dropped the phone back in its cradle and turned to the mirror. I looked at my winged reflection. They were huge. The multicoloured feathers gleamed in the sunlight that streamed into my apartment.

"Well, this complicates things."

This was shaping up to be a situation of craptastic proportions. There was no getting out of this party. If I didn't show up, my Mother would hunt me down, and I still had to pick up a present. Showing up empty-handed was a big no-no in my Mom's world. But the first thing I needed to do was figure out what was going on with my wings.

I made sure the wings were just in my reflection with nothing physically protruding from my back. This involved a five-minute game of peekaboo between me and the mirror. Oh, if my Traveller friends could see me now. I won the game; the wings were just in my reflection, but the funny thing was that the Phoenix in the glass had rips in her shirt where the wings had broken through, but the Phoenix standing in my living room, me, her shirt was intact. Another level of weird in my already strange life.

"Maybe it's just mirrors." I ran to the patio doors to check my reflection there.

I live, well I lived, in a medium-sized loft in an 'up and coming' part of town. FYI, up and coming just means artsy people have moved in and that eventually, one day, it will be a nice place to live. One day. My building was okay, except for Tuesday nights when the apartment below hosted a drum circle.

The bedroom and the bathroom had walls, but the rest of the place was a wide open space. An island separated the kitchen area from the living room, and I'd tried to create more separation by placing a large, complicated looking, bookshelf thing in the middle of the room to house my TV and mass quantities of books. The sheer size of it made a hallway between the kitchen and living room. But the real reason I fell for this place was the balcony and amazing patio doors towards which I was running.

I rushed up to the large stretch of glass and tried to see a ghost of my shape. It was there, or rather, I was there, wings and all, staring back at me. A pale blue silvery self with gossamer wings.

"Ah, crap," I was saying that a lot today.

This complicated things. It hadn't happened last night when I got back; I'd run straight into the bathroom to check, and the mirror was wing free. Why was this happening now? How was I supposed to go to my parents' house when every time I passed a reflective surface my wings were right there in the glass?

"Ah, double crap," I said as I threw open the patio doors and stepped out into warm midday sun.

This was my sanctuary in this world, and it went a long way to explaining the massive greenhouse in my Traveller home. The patio ran the length of the apartment and then wrapped around the corner towards my bedroom window and the fire escape. Over the years I had turned this south facing strip of concrete into a verdant jungle. Bright flowers cascaded from boxes along the entire railing, and a trellis, running up the walls of the building, was covered in vines and climbing roses. Gigantic clay pots played home to large trees that broke up the constant sun that streamed down on the balcony. I'd even set up a mini fountain in the corner, a pillar with a sphere of stone that spun gently on a spray of water. It filled the air with the soft sound of water sliding over stone. It was a little piece of paradise in a big city.

My chaise was calling to me, and I laid out, the sun touching my face dappled by the trees and shrubbery above me. I closed my eyes and thought happy, calming no wings in my reflection thoughts.

2

———

It was around the third... 'Ohm, no wings in my reflection, ohm' that I heard breaking glass coming from my kitchen.

Every inch of my body immediately filled with a buzzing energy. I felt as if I could spring into flight and yet, incredibly; I remained perfectly still. I was calm, deliciously calm and alert. I noticed a warmth at my back and looked over my shoulder to discover my wings had appeared beneath me. They were as soft and strong as I remembered and folded easily against me as I lay on the chaise.

More sounds of destruction filled my ears, and I rolled from the chaise to the floor, my wings tight to my back. Crawling as lithely as a cat, I moved to the patio doors and peeked inside.

There was an enormous creature rummaging through my kitchen drawers. The fridge door was open, and I could see a jar of what looked like mustard, smashed and smeared on the ground. Gross. That would take forever to clean.

"Was that necessary?" I whispered to myself as I reached for the doorknob.

I stopped.

Do I have to reach for the knob, I asked myself. I'm a creature from another dimension, with voyeuristic intentions... I stopped myself from humming the entire Time Warp song... Surely I can get this door to open on its own? I quickly glanced at my intruder, I still couldn't make out who it was, but the big creature was busying itself in my cupboards and seemed fairly preoccupied.

I had a little time to experiment.

I moved back from the door and, making sure I wasn't visible to the creature in the kitchen, knelt facing the knob. I stared at it, hard. Then I stared at it some more, harder.

Nothing happened. Zip. Nada.

"Come on, Phoenix," I sighed and took a deep breath, shaking out my wings like a bird in a bath. The movement sparked a little flame in my heart, and their weight was so comforting I wondered how I ever lived without them. This time, as I looked at the knob, I focused on fanning the flame of the little spark of energy deep inside my body. I had felt how immense it could become weeks earlier, back in the Void. Not only had I blown apart the circle of the Guard, but I had also brought Archer back from certain death. Yes, I was the one who had tried to kill him, but we worked it out.

I focused on that little spark of power, and I breathed life into it. I used my will to make it grow and quickly it was swirling inside me. The green flame coursed through my veins and my wings, soon I thrummed with energy. I rode the vibration. I let it swell and flow through my body until it felt solid in my bones, until it felt like a state of being, always present, woven into the fabric of my soul.

From this place of calm and power, I asked the door to open.

It did.

I rose to my feet. Feeling no fear, only readiness, I stepped through the doorway. In the shadowy kitchen, the creature continued to gorge, stuffing slices of smoked salmon into its mouth. I took a few silent steps forward and called out to it.

"Hello, Yeren."

3

————

She choked on the salmon. I smiled.

"Phoenix! You're here!" She was wiping her hands down her hairy chest, trying to get the mustard and salmon bits from her hands. She merely succeeded in mashing them into her fur. I felt calm and cold as I spoke.

"Of course I'm here. This is my apartment."

The last time I had seen this yeti she was selling me out to my sworn enemies. I wanted to rip her apart with my bare hands. I wanted to launch myself across my apartment and close the fridge door on her head over and over and over and; you get the idea. But she might know where Sid was, and I needed that information before I kicked her ass.

"The real question, Yeren, is how did you get in here?" I opened my wings slightly, she gulped. "I thought Travellers couldn't enter another's home without permission." I cocked my head to the side. "I don't remember giving you permission."

She smiled.

"Well, I guess that means this isn't your home."

I hadn't thought of that. My wings twitched. Her smiled grew broader.

"Why are you here, Yeren?"

"I thought Sid might be here."

"You don't know where he is?"

"No, I've been looking for him everywhere." She was inching her way across the kitchen as she spoke. She didn't think I'd noticed this. I wanted to keep it that way, so I turned easily with her, keeping eye contact. "I thought maybe we could work together and find him quicker." She smiled again, with teeth this time. It was a gruesome sight, bits of salmon and mustard clinging to her bear-like jaws. "That's if you can accept my apology."

"Apology?" I asked quietly. She was up to something, I could feel it. Yeren was trying desperately to shield her energy, but I could sense it welling up inside her.

"Yes, an apology. I'm sorry about how things went down." She held out her hand as if to shake mine. "Friends again?"

I know bullshit when I see it. Fortunately for me, Yeren still thought of me as my former self. The me I was before my time in the mortal world, when I just lived in the Void, quietly healing those who came to me, never making a fuss, keeping to myself. But that was before the inhabitants had come together and banished me in a bloody attack. That was before they sent me screaming into the unknown before I had clawed my way to hell and back to find my wings. That was before. This was now. And Yeren had forgotten all of that.

I slapped an innocent-looking smile on my face and walked towards her.

"I'd like that."

"Great!" She took a step towards me; her smile didn't meet her eyes.

Two things happened at once. Yeren made a grab for me, and I threw a ball of energy at her face. It shot from my hand, a blue-green orb the size of a softball, and hit her right in the nose, sending her slamming back into the kitchen cabinets. She hit them with a loud crack, and the doors fell off the upper units. Blood spurted from her nose, mingling with the mustard and salmon on her fur.

"Bitch! You broke my nose!" she yelled. "Now I am seriously pissed!"

I was already moving; I needed to take cover. I dashed behind the big unit that divided the living room from the kitchen, instinctively tossing another ball of energy over my shoulder as I ran. It hit the island in front of Yeren. Bits of Formica rained down on the apartment. I looked down at my hands.

"How the hell am I doing this?" I whispered to myself.

I had no clue; I had sensed the rising danger in the room, and before I knew what was going on, I'm tossing softballs of destruction all over my apartment. Yeren yelled something incoherent, and a ball of black energy struck two feet above my head.

"Two can play at this game!" she howled. "In fact, I can do this all day! You'll tire soon enough, and then I'll have you."

The black energy oozed like oil, slimy and thick, down my entertainment unit. It hit my television, and it sizzled. The sludge continued to drip down, and I watched as my tv melted. She melted my tv. My beautiful fifty inch HD television. She melted it. The bitch must pay.

I leant around the unit and launched two balls of energy at Yeren in quick succession. One hit the microwave, and the other finished off the upper cabinets that Yeren had already smashed up. Yeren laughed.

"You realize you're just destroying your place, right?"

Damn, she was right; I was trying to force her out of here, and meanwhile, I was just tearing my place apart. There had to be a better way.

"What do you want from me, Yeren?"

She answered without hesitation.

"There's a Bounty on your head, Phoenix. A big Bounty. Every low-life in the Void will be looking for you, but I will be the one that collects."

What the hell was she talking about? As I tried to process her words, a light whooshing sound filled the air, and a giant ball of black crud sailed over the entertainment unit and landed near my feet. I scuttled out of the way as it melted my carpet. This was getting bad. My carpet was melting, and a Bounty was on my head. I had to get out of here and get back to my home, my one true home as it turns out, and regroup with Archer. An experienced warrior like him was just what I needed, but first I wanted to get more information out of Yeren. Even though I could smell my carpet burning, I kept my voice light.

"So is it a 'dead or alive' kind of thing?"

"Oh, they want you alive. Very alive."

"Well, that's comforting. And who is 'they' exactly?"

"No idea."

"That doesn't sound very legit."

"That's how Bounties work in the Void. When I bring you to the meeting place, they will reveal themselves, and I will get my reward."

"What if they don't give you your reward?"

"Then I kill them and you as well for the trouble. How

do humans say it? It's a win-win situation," she laughed. This bitch was crazy; I had to get out of here.

"What's the reward?" I tried to sound blasé even though the patch of black ooze next to me was creeping closer.

"Why do you care?"

"Well, if it was really cool, like a dirt bike or something, maybe I turn myself in, and we split it."

She laughed.

"You can't split power."

"Power? That's it?" the disbelief was plain in my voice. "More power?"

"Not just power," she scoffed. "That would be meaning-less. The creature that brings you in gets a share of your power."

"Seriously? You guys already tried that," I sighed heavily, dramatically, letting boredom coat my voice. "Remember? You ripped off my wings and sent me flying?"

I could feel my wings reacting to the tale. Power rippled through my feathers. The air around me felt charged, like the sky before a lightning storm.

"Nobody got a piece of me then," I called out. "And nobody's getting a piece of me now."

My power was growing. Yeren was forced to shout her retort above the rushing winds of energy that now filled the apartment.

"Not this time, Phoenix! The news has Travelled through the Void like wildfire! There is a creature who has figured out how to strip you of your power! They have mastered how to take all that you are! You cannot stop them! They will take your precious wings for good, and I will share in the spoils!"

Seething with rage, I burst from behind the cabinet as Yeren threw a giant ball of pulsating blackness towards me. I threw up my hands to shield myself from the evil tar hurtling towards me. As the word shield flitted through my mind, a shimmery wall of energy materialized before me. The ball of darkness hit the shield and rebounded towards Yeren. I watched through the shimmering veil as it hit her full on in the chest and ate away at her fur.

She screamed.

I Travelled.

4

I landed on my ass in the middle of the forest path that led to my home. A quick flap of my wings brought me to my feet, and I started down the path. I guess this truly was home now. I couldn't go back to my apartment since it was no longer safe, but I needed to maintain some home base in that time. Maybe Archer knew some protection magic that I could use on the place. The Archer. The thought of him quickened my heart. He said he would be waiting for me when I returned and that reunion couldn't come soon enough. Now that there was a Bounty on my head, I needed him more than ever. I half ran, half flew, along the path.

Three creatures that had permission to enter my home; Archer, Benyst and Noiryn. They were my three most trusted friends in this strange world. Well, Archer was more than a friend, but we hadn't labelled our relationship.

Noiryn is a beautiful, blue scaled Siren at home on land and sea, and Benyst is, well honestly I don't know what Benyst is. His appearance is quite startling at first; large fleshy growths that seem to pulse and change from time to time cover his body. He's a little reclusive and grumpy, but underneath the rough exterior is a real softy. Without him and Noiryn, I would never have found my wings.

I passed through the archway of trees that formed the energy gate to my home. To me, it felt like moving through a misty waterfall, to an intruder it would feel like a million electric eels wriggling on their skin. Excellent protection.

A broad green lawn spread out before me, just as thick and lush as the first time I saw it. The massive stone house I called home was perfectly nestled in the tree framed clearing. Sun glinted off the roof of the massive greenhouse that comprised an entire wing of the home. It felt so good to see the solid stone and glass and green welcoming me.

In the openness of the garden, I could fully spread my wings, and I crossed the yard in a few energetic flaps. The two stone gargoyles that sat either side of the entry seemed to welcome me as I stopped before the great wooden doors and threw them open.

"Archer?" I called out. "Archer?"

I ran into the living room; it was empty. Well, it was full of amazing things like dinosaur bones and giant seashells, but no Archer. I went over to the fireplace where we'd been sitting before I'd left. The ashes were cold. "Archer?" I called more loudly now, panic slowly edging its way into my voice. The house was silent.

I crossed to the other side of the home and into the greenhouse. The lush plants reached for the sky, and humidity clung to my skin. I called for him and again was met by silence. Back in the great hall, I used my wings to my make quick work of the stairs. I ran down the second-floor hallway, calling his name over and over. I burst into my room, expecting to see him lying on the bed, but it was empty. My fear was growing as I hurried back down the stairs. I was in danger, and I needed to find him. I ran out the main doors into the garden. I stood on the steps and called his name.

"Archer?"

"He's not here," said a gravelly voice behind me. I yelped and spun towards the sound.

A stone gargoyle was smiling at me. It had shifted from its stately perch and sat back on its heels, looking up at me with eyes that were opaque orbs of jet black stone.

"Hello, I'm Grog," said the gargoyle.

"And I'm Brog."

A second, slightly higher, gravelly voice had me spinning again. The stone gargoyle on the other side of the entryway was also smiling at me. Of course, I thought to myself, how stupid of me, of course, they would both talk. My life made Alice in Wonderland look normal.

"I'm Phoenix."

"We know!" said Brog, rather exuberantly.

"Quiet down," Grog replied, "You're talking too loud again."

"Oh! Sorry!" cried Brog, realising he was still shouting, his stony ears flattened, and he whispered. "Sorry." As his ears moved, I noticed a sizeable chunk of stone was missing from the top of his skull. Grog saw me looking.

"Yep, dropped on his head when he was just a little pebble."

"Right," I said the word slowly, drawing out the vowel, maybe if I didn't finish it, I wouldn't have to deal with the fact that two stone gargoyles were talking to me. But really, after everything I'd been through, this was low on the weird list. I finished the word with a crisp little 't', shook off the shock and addressed the gargoyles.

"So, Grog, Brog, how come you've never talked to me before?"

"This is the first time you've been here alone," Brog replied.

"Well, miss," Grog continued, "what Brog is trying to say is; we are your guardian gargoyles, no one else's. So we can only appear to you."

"Okay," I was getting superb at just going with things. "How did you get here?"

"You saved us!" Brog shouted.

"I did?" I had no memory of doing such a thing. I guess this was something else my wings had still to reveal to me.

"My brother is correct. You brought us here from our crumbling cathedral. Although we could not speak to you until you had made this place truly our home, you sensed our true nature and brought us here. We are very grateful and loyal servants."

They bowed to me. Grog was elegant on his powerful stone legs and his tail extended out behind him as he bent forward, nose almost touching the ground. Brog had a bit of trouble keeping his balance. This could have been because of his short stubby tail, but it was more likely because he couldn't stop smiling at me. I looked at that goofy stone smile, and my wings twitched as a memory flashed through my mind.

I was in a dark, dusty place; large wooden beams laid haphazardly around me, some angled up, still attached to the roof above. Sharp shafts of sunlight broke through the walls and in their sparkling light, dust moved like diamonds caught in the air. I moved forward, my wings dragging ever so slightly in the dust, picking my way through the debris, not searching for anything in particular, just exploring this old forgotten place. I came across a compact turret room that jutted out from the primary space. A colossal beam had fallen across the entrance, and I had to flap my wings to rise above it into the alcove beyond.

Once inside, I discovered a curving stone staircase that rose into the darkness above. The first few stairs were crumbling rubble, and although the space was too small for flight, I used short flaps of my wings to help me as I scrambled up the rocky incline to the solid stairs above. I climbed slowly, gingerly, in the near pitch black, running my hands along the walls, taking each step one at a time so I could test its strength. I climbed for some time, always curving to the right, the darkness and motion making me queasy.

Thin shafts of light broke through and soon the stairs opened up to a small landing and a thick wooden door. I pushed on the door, and it fell forward with a loud bang. The room beyond was now nothing more than a large platform open to the elements. The remnants of once opulent furniture were strewn about. A threadbare carpet lay mouldering on the floor. A wardrobe lay on its side, wide open and empty. A shredded pile of cotton was all that was left of the bed. A wasted journey, I thought, and with a heavy sigh, I turned to head back downstairs. I had my foot on the first step when I realised I could simply fly from the open room.

As I turned back, I saw them. Huddled on either side of the doorway were two small stone gargoyles, I had missed them in the half-light before I opened the door. I went to the first one; a sizeable chunk of stone was missing from its head. I placed my hand on the stone, and it tingled. I gasped and pulled my hand away. I went to the second gargoyle and placed my hand on its head. This time the tingling was much stronger. There was some power in these stone figures. I knelt between the two statues and placed a hand on each carved figure. Power flowed through me from the two statues; it felt good, strong and clean like I had connected a well-designed circuit. I slowly dragged my hands away; I could have sworn I felt the one with the chunk missing move. I looked back and forth between the gargoyles and smiled.

"Well, I can't leave you here, can I?"

5
______

I was back in reality; Grog was dabbing at my hand with his icy stone claws.

"Miss?"

"Sorry, I was having a flashback," I murmured. "I brought you here one at a time."

"You brought me here first," Brog said proudly.

"And we have stood guard for you ever since," Grog added as he settled back onto his perch.

"And how long is that exactly?" I asked the pair.

"I'm sorry, miss, we have no relationship with Time."

"Right." I had to get moving again. This conversation was eating up a lot of time, time I needed to use getting prepared for Bounty hunters. "Now, a question for you; where is the Archer?"

"Oh-oh-oh!" Brog was waving his hand in the air like a desperate middle school kid that finally had the right answer.

"Yes, Brog?"

"He left!" he shouted and then clapped his hands over

his mouth, trying to contain the loud sound. Brog was cute, a little annoying, but still cute.

"Okay, did he say where he was going?"

Brog raised his hand again, but Grog jumped in.

"No, miss. He does not know of our true nature so he would say nothing to us."

"Okay," I was getting ticked, my general fear coping mechanism. "When did he leave?"

"We have no..." Grog began.

"Relationship with time," I finished.

I stood there thinking. Archer would come back; the question was when. In the meantime, did I want to sit here waiting for him? I needed to get some answers to the many questions swirling around my head, and if Archer couldn't give them to me, I'd have to go to my other sources, Benyst and Noiryn. I needed to figure things out fast; I still had a birthday party to go to.

"All right guys, if Archer comes back, tell him..." Grog interrupted me.

"We cannot reveal ourselves to him, miss," he looked crestfallen, "I wish that we could."

"Sorry, Grog, I forgot. It's no problem, I'll catch up with him eventually, but I have to say bye for now because I have to get going." I started walking down the steps.

"In your pyjamas?" Brog asked.

I looked down at myself. I was indeed in my pyjamas and not much pyjama at that. A simple pair of cotton shorts, well, short-shorts really, and a tank top were the only things keeping me from naked. I then remembered I hadn't brushed my teeth or my hair that morning either. Energy battles with big bad yetis can preoccupy a girl.

"Good question, Brog. I think I'll go change." I dashed

back into the house, using my wings to get me to my bedroom in record time.

I burst into my room and headed straight for the three gigantic oak closets that lined an entire wall of the space. I pulled open the doors of each closet and surveyed my options.

The clothing here was all from my Traveller life, and in that life, I'd had a major penchant for catsuits. Although, I imagined I called them bird-suits, you know, because of the wings. I also liked black. A lot of black. Ninety-eight percent of the jumpsuits here were black, and the other two percent were crazy bright colours like lime green and fuchsia. No way was I going out in one of those. I pulled off my shorts since the tank wouldn't go over my wings I had to rip it off, which took a while.

"This is what happens when you don't plan ahead, Phoenix," I said to myself as the last bit of fabric tore free.

I moved to the first wardrobe and pulled out a bra and panties. I hadn't been able to wear a bra with the suit I'd worn when I'd first got here, but I'd since found a few catsuits in this closet that I could accommodate one. Not a regular bra, mind you. It needed to be strapless to accommodate the other set of girls at my back, but it was better than nothing.

I went to the second wardrobe and pulled out one of the many, many, many black catsuits. This one had panels that went over my shoulders, crossed in the back and then wrapped around my torso to tie in the front. The trick was getting the cross right between my wings. There was a full-length mirror on the inside of the closet door, and I checked myself out. Everything seemed in place. I reached into the bottom of the wardrobe and pulled out my favourite pair of black leather boots. I'd gotten them when I was a straight up human, but they worked great with the wardrobe I'd found here.

I then moved to the third closet. This is the one I'd spent the least amount of time exploring. When I'd first arrived at the house, I'd opened every cabinet in the place, excited by the possibilities of this new wardrobe. This one had appeared to be just outerwear, so I'd moved on, but now I needed to find something to keep me warm and tone things down when I got back on human time. I didn't want to be walking around in just a catsuit. It's a hard look to pull off in day-to-day life.

I ran my hands over the pieces of clothing stuffed into the closet. Fur, felt, and wool touched my hands. There were many colours; black, of course, and various shades of green, purple and blue. My eyes caught something shimmering and my hands stopped. I pulled the shimmering wonder from the mass of coats and looked at closely. It was a beautiful swing coat the colour of the night sky. Literally, the night sky. The shimmering was a smattering of stars that covered the garment in groupings like the Milky Way, hints of pink and green running through them. I had to try this on.

I stepped back from the wardrobe so I could see myself better in the glass, and I swung the coat over my head. The stars shifted slightly as the light fabric dropped around me. My wings seemed to remember the garment, and they compressed themselves into lengthy lines that slipped through slits that fit perfectly around their bases, leaving them unencumbered. My arms found themselves draped with long open sleeves; they could move freely, uncovered, in front of me or slip into the fabric panels at my sides. It was more cape than coat, hitting me at mid-thigh with an interior drawstring that cinched and defined my waist. It had a slight cowl neckline that fastened with a large pewter button. The dark navy galaxy made my multicoloured wings appear to float in infinity. It looked fabulous.

"Wow," I whispered. The old me had great taste.

I shook myself from my reverie and dashed into the bathroom. I quickly brushed everything, teeth, hair, the usual, and rushed back outside.

Grog and Brog were waiting for me. I called out my goodbyes as I flew across the garden.

"See you soon, boys!"

"Be safe, miss." Grog called. Brog was waving enthusiastically.

"Bye! I like your coat!"

I turned and smiled at him as I dropped low to pass through the gate. I ran down the path to the spot I could Travel from and thinking furiously of Benyst's jungle hideaway; I jumped into Time itself.

6

———

I landed on my feet. I think I am getting better at this non-human thing.

I was in the middle of a large clearing. Torches flickered around the perimeter and beyond them was an impenetrable jungle. Benyst's modest hut stood in the middle of the clearing. I looked up, taking in the star-filled sky above me. It always seemed to be night here. It was a peaceful and secluded spot yet with the jungle surrounding it; it held an undercurrent of raw power.

"Phoenix!"

A woman's light voice sounded from inside the hut. I turned in time to see a curtain fall back into place as the sound of footfalls filled the clearing. Noiryn was here too, interesting.

"It is so good to see you!"

She bounded around the hut and across the grass towards me. Noiryn was as lithe and graceful as the last time I'd seen her, which come to think of it was only a week ago. Time is hard to keep track of when you're moving between worlds. The blue scales that covered her body shone in the torchlight and her third eye was open and bright. That was new. The last time I'd seen her, it blinked from time to time, but nothing more. Very interesting. She threw her arms around me, and we held each other like it had been years since we'd seen each other.

"Noiryn, I'm glad you're here. I was hoping to see you both."

She stepped back from me, a big smile on her strangely beautiful fish mouth.

"I've been spending a lot of time here lately," she whispered, excitement clear in her tone. "Wait till you see Benyst."

"I heard that!" a gruff voice called. I looked up to see Benyst coming towards us.

At least I thought it was Benyst. The last time I had seen him, his face had been a distorted mask of tumours and growths. His forehead had hung heavy over his eyes, his lips distended like pink plantains, and his arms and hands had been lumpy in the extreme. But now his growths had reduced dramatically in size. Yes, there was still some deformity, but the shape of his face was more visible. His lips had shrunk considerably, his arms looked smoother, and I could actually see his eyes.

"Amazing," I breathed out the word, and my wings unfurled with the sound.

"Oh, don't go getting excited," Benyst waved at my wings, a smile on his renewed lips. "It was bound to happen sometime."

He winked at Noiryn. She giggled. My brain melted.

"Whoa, are you two..." I let the question hang in the air as I looked back and forth between them. Benyst held out his arm, and Noiryn tucked underneath it, wrapping her arms around his waist.

"It's early days yet."

She smiled. He smiled. They smiled at each other.

"Wow, that's awesome guys. You make a cute couple."

And it was, and they did. There was something about Benyst's gruff nature and Noiryn's soft heart that seemed right together. In the torchlight, I could almost see their energies intertwining. Her blue softening his red, as his red intensified her blue. As I watched them stare into each other's eyes, I could almost see Benyst's face reforming.

"So why is your face changing?" Benyst appreciated blunt.

"Ah," he sighed, pulling from their embrace, but keeping hold of Noiryn's hand. "That is a mystery for another day."

Translation: I'm not talking about this right now, Phoenix. To say Benyst valued his privacy was an understatement. The guy had spent thirty years alone in his jungle hideaway. I wondered if Noiryn knew what was going on. Not that I'd try to pump her for information or anything.

"Cool, another day it is then."

"So what brings you here, Phoenix? Or is this just a friendly visit?" Noiryn asked.

"Ah, she just likes my stew," Benyst grunted. "Come on ladies, let's eat!" He turned and headed back around the hut with Noiryn by his side and me trailing behind them.

"Actually," I said, trying to be nonchalant. "I found out there's a Bounty out on me."

They both froze in mid-stride and then spoke at once.

"Bounty?" Noiryn asked.

"What the hell!?" Benyst exclaimed.

They peppered me with questions, not giving me time to understand what they were saying, let alone answer. I could hear the fear in their voices, a fear I hadn't yet allowed myself to feel. And anger. Benyst was so angry. His rough voice pounded through the clearing like boulders sliding down a mountainside. I could feel my stress levels rising and with it, my power. I knew if I didn't stop their energetic avalanche soon, I would explode. I threw up my hands and unfurled my wings, letting the buildup of power pour out their tips in a rain of sparks as I bellowed.

"Enough!" They stopped talking. I took a few deep breaths. "I'm sorry, I have only just found out..."

Benyst cut me off.

"We better get inside. Now."

7

Benyst grabbed Noiryn and me by the wrist and led us quickly into the hut. He shoved us both through the hut's door and closed it behind us, whispering an incantation as he did so.

"We should be safe now."

"Benyst," I was trying hard to contain myself. "I don't care what is happening; never pull me around like that again. Ever."

I held his gaze. For a moment he looked as if he would argue with me, then he thought better of it.

"Sorry." That was big for him.

"Thanks." I released the breath I was holding.

He nodded, but at that moment something had changed between us. When we had first met, I was alone and scared, powerless in a world full of incredible creatures out for my blood. But now I was stronger, now I had both my wings, and even though I couldn't control all my powers, I was a lot better at kicking ass. Something we'd both have to get used to.

"How did you find out?" Noiryn asked, trying to ease the

tension as she gestured for me to take a seat by the hut's central fire.

"Yeren told me."

"Yeren?!" they chorused.

"Yep, told me as she was lobbing balls of corrosive black ooze around my apartment."

"Your apartment back in your old time?" Noiryn asked.

"Yes, I guess Sid must have told her where it was."

Sid. I wish that had turned out better.

"But you're a Traveller, how did she get in without permission?" Noiryn leaned forward in her chair, her third eye looking me up and down.

"Well, as she pointed out, it must not be my home anymore."

Saying the words out loud hurt. If that place was no longer my home, then I had truly left that life behind. It was where my family was, well, my post Void, pre-wing family; the people who had raised me. How was I going to let that go? I could feel tears welling up and decided that it was a question better answered later. Much later.

"What did she say about the Bounty?" Benyst's voice was a quiet growl. I couldn't tell if he was pissed at me or the Bounty itself. I'm going with Bounty.

"She said that a creature in the Void had promised a share of my power to whoever brought me to them alive."

"Ha!" Benyst laughed. "They already tried that! And look where it got them! A useless Bounty if ever there was one."

Behaving as if the matter was closed, Benyst got to his feet and ladled stew from the cast-iron pot that was bubbling above the fire. I kept talking.

"She said that this creature had figured out what went wrong the last time. She said that they knew how to strip me of my power. And..." I sighed. "I believe her."

Silence met my words. Only the sound of soup dripping from the ladle Benyst held poised above the fire filled the space.

"Did she say where the meeting place was?"

"Nope. She wouldn't tell me who had put it out on me, either."

"Well, that's how Bounties work in the Void. Anonymous until the last." Benyst resumed pouring stew into bowls.

So Yeren had told me the truth about Void Bounty protocol. Great.

"What does the Archer say about all this?"

Benyst shoved a bowl of stew in my hands as he spoke. It smelled amazing. My stomach growled. I hadn't had breakfast and scared or not; I was going to eat. Noiryn passed me a spoon, and I tucked in.

"That's the other problem," I said between mouthfuls. "I can't find him. He was supposed to be at my place when I returned, but I came back sooner than scheduled. I guess he went out or something."

I was about to mention that my gargoyles didn't know where he'd gone, but kept their existence to myself. I trusted Noiryn and Benyst, it just felt like something I needed to keep to myself for a while.

"Why didn't you go to his home?" Noiryn asked.

"Well, this is kind of embarrassing," I put down my empty bowl. "Wow, I inhaled that," Benyst grunted approvingly. "I don't know where his home is, I've never been there."

Yes, I have never seen my boyfriend's place. I know, I know, red flag. Seriously though, I hadn't really cared before now. I'd asked to see it, and he'd said he wanted to wait until I was stronger because it was a hard place to Travel to. That was all right with me. Until now. Now I wished I could show up, kick the door down and demand he take care of me. Yes, I'm complicated.

"That's not embarrassing," Noiryn said, "I've heard it's very hard to Travel to."

"You think I like my privacy," Benyst chuckled.

"Well, I have to find him. I need his help to figure out who put this Bounty out on me and what the hell I'm going to do about it." I stood up. "But first I have to go to a birthday party."

"A what?!" My friends were getting magnificent at speaking in unison.

"A birthday party for my brother." I slapped a hand to my forehead. "And I need to get him a present! Shit!" I slapped my other hand to my forehead. "I have no freaking cash on me, and I can't go back to my place and get my purse. Triple shit."

"Jeez, girl, you're a Traveller! With all that power at your fingertips, you can't get some cash?" Benyst was smiling; it was strange to see his lips so small.

"I'm not robbing someone, Benyst."

Benyst laughed outright.

"Rob someone! You couldn't do that if you tried, not in your nature." He wiped tears of mirth from his cheeks, a much easier task now they were smoother. "Just bewitch one of those money dispenser thingies."

"Money dispenser? Oh, an ATM! I hadn't thought of that. That might work. Excellent idea." It would be harder than opening a door with my powers, but I think I could manage it. I moved to leave. "I'll go do what I need to do in my old time and then head back here."

"And while you're gone, we'll see what we can find out about this Bounty," Noiryn looked concerned but hopeful as she crossed the room to embrace me. As we hugged her hands brushed my wings and the question, I'd completely forgotten came hurtling to through my mind.

"Shit!" Noiryn jumped back. "Sorry, Noiryn. I just remembered a huge question I had to ask you guys. Well, not really a question, more of a concern I need input on..."

"Spit it out, Phoenix," Noiryn said, Benyst was rubbing off on her.

"In my old time, when my wings are away, I can still see them in my reflection." They both just looked at me. "I can't go around like that! What will people think when I'm walking down the street? What will my parents say?"

"Oh!" It looked like a light bulb when off in Noiryn's brain. "You're worried that people will see them."

"Yeah, that seems like a problem, no?" I countered.

"Don't worry, Phoenix, only Travellers, will see the reflection and most won't be looking for it."

"Oh, that's a relief."

"But," Benyst interjected, "with the Bounty out, they will be more observant than usual. So take care."

"I will. Wait a second, how come I didn't see the wings when I first got back to my old time. I looked for them, but they weren't in my reflection."

Benyst thought about this.

"I don't know. Maybe you were tired. I wouldn't worry about it."

"Okay...." That was not as reassuring as I'd hoped.

Benyst raised his arm and appeared to wipe the air in front of the doorway clean. The energy shield he'd put up dropped, and I slipped out of the hut.

"See you soon," I called over my shoulder.

I moved to the centre of the clearing and thought of a place in my old time, a busy street a few blocks from my home where I could get a gift for my brother.

"Seriously," I grumbled to myself. "I'm a freaking Traveller, every creature in the Void is trying to hunt me down, and I've got to go to a birthday party. When do the perks kick in?"

My wings, that still seemed from time to time to operate independently of me, flapped and pull me up into the air. I hovered ten feet above the ground.

"Oh yeah, this is pretty perky."

I smiled to myself and Travelled.

8

I landed on my feet again. Yay, me! I was getting so much better at that. The first thing that hit me was a smell, a putrid and foul, bring up your breakfast kind of smell. I inhaled and was instantly coated inside and out with it. Trying not to gag, I looked around for the source of the offensive order. It was easy to find. I had arrived in my old Time in a secluded alley, right next to an overflowing dumpster. Spoiled food was cascading over the sides, and the main contents had liquefied. As I looked in horror at the filthy pile, a small squeaking sound met my ears. I looked down to find a big fat greasy rat sniffing at my shoe. I panicked, screamed and kicked the thing halfway down the alley. It landed on its back, righted itself, looked backed and half squeaked, half screamed at me, and then ran away. I stifled a need to vomit and hastily performed the bit of power weaving that made my wings disappear and made me visible to the surrounding humans. It was a little harder than usual, what with the smell of rotting meat filling my head holes, but I managed it.

I did my patented slow dog chasing her tail move to

make sure the wings were truly out of sight then sprinted out of the alley. I glanced left and right to get my bearings, then headed south towards Jones Street. I had landed right where I wanted; on a busy street with a good mix of soccer moms, teens on their cell phones, and hipsters.

I got to Jones and immediately crossed, heading for the bank a few stores down. A woman sat on the steps with a sign that said: "My kids are hungry." She looked up at me as approached the door.

"Spare any change, miss?"

"Give me a minute." I smiled at her and entered the bank.

Fortunately, the bank was closed, and the small glassed-in room with the ATMs was empty. As I looked around, I noticed my reflection blazing on nearly every surface. Each image had giant multicoloured wings hanging from its back. Sigh. I hoped Benyst was right.

I walked up to the ATM farthest from the door and, for the benefit of the security cameras, put my hand in my pocket and then withdrew it, pretending to put a bank card in the machine. Then I stood there for a second, thinking. When I had opened the door at my apartment, I had stoked my power and asked the door to open. I figured it would be the same procedure here, it would just need more power.

"More power!" I said to the ATM in what I thought was a convincing Scottish brogue.

I raised my palm before the ATM keypad and brought my power to the surface. This time the power within me swirled red and fiery. It moved like lava and flames as it licked its way through my body, up my torso, through my mind, answering my request, and down my arm and into my outstretched fingers. Red lightning slipped from my finger-tips to zap the control pad, and the thing whirled to life. I held my hand in place as the screen flashed through the usual commands, my power coaxing it along. The screen asking me how much to withdraw flashed up and before I could answer it was gone. Flash flash flash went the remaining prompts and suddenly the words 'thank you' appeared. I heard gears moving inside the machine, and it expelled a wad of cash. I grabbed the cash, and with it, my power receded. I looked at the money in my hand. It was a lot.

There had to be a couple thousand in my hands. I didn't have that kind of money in my account. Oh shit, I was stealing. Not wanting to be on camera any more than I had to, I peeled off and few hundred-dollar bills and put the remaining bills in an interior pocket of my coat. I left the bank and sat down with the woman on the stairs.

"Here you go." I handed her what I could now see was five hundred dollars. She took the bills and counted them, a look of suspicion on her face. "Don't worry about it," I stood up and brushed off my pants. "It's cool," I said, trying not to look guilty, and hurried down the street before she could ask questions.

Man, I felt guilty. I had just stolen a lot of money from a bank. If they ever caught me, I was going to jail big time. Remembering at that point that I was a Traveller and really wouldn't ever have to go to jail, quelled my fear, but not my guilt. When this Bounty situation was resolved, I'd have to figure out some kind of money source. Maybe I could Travel back in time and invest in something, set up some offshore accounts or whatever people with big money do. Another problem for another day.

While I had been contemplating my possible incarceration, my feet had taken me to Jones Video, the cool indie DVD place in my neighbourhood. My brother has a thing for Japanese horror films. I don't know much about the genre, mainly because I'm not good with horror movies, I get nightmares, big time, screaming myself awake nightmares, but I knew this place had a good selection for sale. I'd just pick one at random and hope for the best. All I knew for sure was he had Ichi the Killer.

I entered the store and went straight to the back where the harder stuff was shelved. I tried not to look at the various gory covers as I grabbed one at random, made sure it wasn't Ichi, I think it said Audition, and got the hell out of there. Yes, I'm a wuss with horror films, even the covers gross me out. I can take on the Guard and battle with a Yeti, but simulated violence makes me feel nauseous.

I got to the register and put the DVD on the counter face down. As I reached into my pocket to pull out some cash, I noticed my reflection in the mirror behind the clerk. My wings were vibrant, stretched out to their full length in the mirror world before me. Holy shit. I was about to say a thank you for the lack of Travellers in the vicinity when I heard a gasp behind me. I whirled around to meet my attacker and saw nothing but racks of movies before me.

"You okay?" the clerk asked.

"Yeah," I took a long look at the store, nothing. I turned back to him, "These movies just get me spooked."

"Even the covers? That's hilarious."

He laughed at me while he rang in my purchase. Normally I would have torn a strip off the guy, but I was preoccupied with discovering the source of that gasp. Not wanting to turn around again, I scanned the store using the mirror in front of me. As I distractedly handed over a fifty, a slight shuffling sound caught my attention. It sounded low to the ground, and I subtly rose on my toes to see the floor of the store in the mirror.

There on the ground, beneath a tower of romantic comedies, was a minion I did not recognise. He was trying to free his foot, which had gotten stuck in the rack. I cleared my throat. The minion looked up with a start and our eyes locked.

"Gotcha," I whispered.

9

"What was that, Ma'am?"

I glanced at the clerk, and the minion grabbed the opportunity. He ripped his foot from the shelf and dashed out of the store. I made to chase it, and the clerk stopped me.

"Ma'am, your DVD!"

"Right," I grabbed the bag he was holding out towards me. "Thanks." I took another step towards the door.

"Your change!"

"Keep it!" I shouted back to him as I raced for the door.

I stepped out into the bright sunlight of the street just in time to see the minion scrambling down the sidewalk. He moved with a similar gait to Sid, hands and feet propelling him forward. He was also just as good as Sid at weaving around obstacles. I gave chase as I watched him dash around strollers and skateboards; a small dog in a pink coat sensed his presence and tried to snap at him as he passed. The minion gave it a quick bop on the nose and kept moving. The dog whimpered and was immediately picked up by its fussy owner. As I passed, the owner gave my coat a half impressed, half bitchy once over. To be fair, I did the same with her boots, which were awesome knee high grey suede, but I digress.

I followed the minion around a corner and into the alley, then I brought forth my wings, rendering me invisible to people on the street. I heard a little boy call out, "Where'd that lady go?" and an angry "Come along, Jeffrey!" as I ventured down the alley.

I found the minion at the end of the alleyway, hidden behind some boxes. Only the curve of his back was visible to me, and it forcibly reminded me of finding Sid in my apartment what seemed like a lifetime ago. The small creature was shaking and breathing hard as he attempted to hide. I stood before the boxes and positioned myself to stop any attempts he might make to escape.

"Who are you?" I asked the quivering form.

"Ah!" he yelped.

"Seriously? You didn't know I was standing right here? Or you didn't think I'd actually speak to you?"

One little grey-brown hand reached over the edge of the box, followed by the top of a tiny head and two enormous moist grey eyes. He coughed a little before he spoke.

"You're not going to attack me?"

"I'm not in the habit of beating on creatures I know nothing about." I gave the minion my straightest 'don't mess with me' face. It gulped, audibly. "Why don't you come out from behind those boxes and tell me who you are and why you're following me."

The creature crawled over the side of the box and sat on its lid. He, and I say he because I've never even heard of a she-minion, was smaller than Sid and no power radiated from him. Whereas Sid's face had been gorilla meets human, this little guy had more of tiny monkey vibe to his visage. He seemed harmless enough, but I'd learnt the hard way not to take harmless at face value. Baba Yaga, anyone?

"Name?"

"Tog." The creature stretched out the sound like a sigh.

"Okay, Tog, why are you following me?"

"Sid asked me to check on you."

"Sid!" I quickly stepped forward, and Tog shot behind the box. I steadied myself. "Sorry, Tog, you just caught me off guard. Please come out."

"You have a lot of energy," Tog mused wearily as he crawled up on the box again.

"So I've heard." I crouched down, my wings stretching slightly for balance. "Is Sid okay?"

"Well, sort of. He's still running, but our leader has not found him yet."

"Greldrom is looking for him?"

"Yes, ma'am." Why was everyone calling me ma'am today? I've barely passed 30; maybe I need more sleep or something.

"So Big G is looking for him because of what happened with me in the Circle, yes?"

"Big G?"

"Greldrom."

"Oh!" Tog giggled. A very slurpy experience. "That's funny. Yes, that's why Big G is looking for him."

"Right, so where is Sid?"

"I can't tell you." Tog looked scared.

"Why not?" Yeah, it came out a little more sharply than was warranted.

"He asked me not to." Tog bowed his head. "I'm sorry."

"That's okay, Tog." I sat on a clean-ish looking box next to him. "Did he say why?" Tog shook his head no.

One day I would find Sid and work things out. He may

have been the one who told the Guard about me healing other creatures, which led to my Banishment, but he had been such an excellent friend and had worked so hard to make up for selling me out. Without him, I would still live my human life with no idea who I truly was. I would always love Sid for that. I swiped at the tears that were brimming at the edges of my eyes and turned my attention back to Tog.

"So, Tog, if you can't tell me about Sid, can you tell me something about this Bounty that's on my head?" Tog sat up very straight, his ears pointing to the sky.

"You know?" he asked.

"Yep."

"But you're so calm."

"Yep."

"And you're outside, alone?"

"Is that bad?" A growing sense of concern was building in the pit of my stomach. "I figured I was okay in my old Time since few creatures knew of it."

"Ma'am, when you fought off Big G your power went screaming through the Void. Every creature within its undulating lands tasted you that day. With a little perseverance, any of them could track you down."

"Oh." Shit. "But do they know about the Bounty?"

"Most do," Tog nodded sadly. "Big G told all of us Minions and offered a separate reward to any of his subjects who bring you to him." He looked me straight in the eyes. "You must be careful. Anyone could be after you."

There was a tension in his voice that had not been there before. I rose to my feet and moved to the other side of the alley, keeping my eyes on him as I moved.

"Don't go getting any ideas, Tog."

"Oh, I couldn't take you," he smiled. "But I have friends who could."

"Did Sid really send you to check on me?" I asked, waiting for the other shoe to drop.

"Well, it's sort of funny really," Tog's demeanour changed as he spoke, gone was the weak, shaky Minion. "You see, Sid was talking in his sleep," Tog smiled, I saw teeth this time. Long, pointy teeth. "I guess my friends and I had tired him out with all our... questioning. And he kept going on about a particular time."

Tog laughed and took a step towards me. Man, I fell hard for his weak little Minion act. Why am I so gullible?

"At first we thought he was just delirious, but the Time never changed." Tog looked around. "Yes, he mentioned it very clearly over and over. So I was dispatched to see if there was any validity to his ramblings." Tog looked me up and down, now only a few feet away. "And there is, for here you are. I can't wait to tell the others." There was that creepy smile again. "And Big G."

I had to get out of here. And stop Tog from talking.

"You didn't count on one thing, Tog."

"Oh?" His enormous eyes widened in mock interest. "What's that?"

"My head start."

I think he sensed the general idea of what I was about to do a nanosecond before I did it. Unfortunately for him, he thought it would involve power, and he raised a hand to block my energy. I knew he'd be expecting this, so I went for the good old human approach. I kicked him in the crotch.

Okay, he didn't have much of a crotch, and with his height, my kick looked more like a dance move than something you'd use in a fight, but it did the trick. Tog dropped like a stone. As he went down, I twisted my body, using my wings for balance, as I drove my fist into the back of his head. His skull bounced hard off the pavement, and he was out cold. The entire thing took about three seconds.

I checked to see if he was still breathing. He was. I dragged him over to the pile of boxes. Yeah, I could have easily carried him, but dragging him across the garbage-strewn alley seemed appropriate. And I swear, there was no way to avoid that puddle.

I opened one of the boxes, it was full of old newspapers; I tossed Tog roughly inside and then covered him with the paper. I closed the box and put it back with the others.

"That should buy me some time," I hid my wings and ran the three blocks to my car.

I got to my little hatchback, had the door open and was in my seat before I realised I had locked the car and I had no keys.

"Wow," I mused, tossing the bag with the DVD onto the seat beside me. "I'm getting better at this stuff." I pointed a finger at the ignition. "Go!" I said with a smile, and the car rumbled into life. I put the car in drive and turned on the radio.

Time to go to a party!

My life is so strange.

10

I'd become accustomed to the speed of time travel, so the drive felt incredibly long. But I couldn't very well arrive at my parents' house on foot. That would definitely raise some eyebrows.

I got to the house, and the driveway was full. Great, everybody's already here, I grumbled as I parked on the street. It would mean more people to distract my mother though, which was a good thing.

I grabbed the DVD, ripped off the price tag, and walked up the driveway. I spied the new 'baby on board' sticker on my sister, Cat's, car. "Took her long enough," I mumbled. "Jen is nine months old." My niece is the cutest baby ever. Not that I'm biased or anything. My sister and her husband both have jet black hair, as does everyone in my family except me, and my little niece has a big head of ebony curls. It is stupid adorable.

The warmth of the house engulfed me as I slipped through the door and I could see my family down the hall, gathered in the kitchen as always.

"Hello!" I made my way to the brightly lit room.

"Phoenix!"

It was a chorus in the Greek tradition as every member of my family said my name at approximately the same time with varying degrees of enthusiasm.

"Hey, guys!" I replied, hoping to match their energy.

Then the hugging started.

Besides my brother, I have three sisters who are all married, and all have children. So there were many people to greet. It went by in the same blur it always does. Up first, my sister Lauren, who is only two years younger than me, her husband Ted and their three kids. All boys. The three terrors, so named for a good reason, said fast hellos and jetted back to the basement playroom. Lauren and Ted went back to their Scrabble game with my Dad, who waved jovially at me. Jim, my sister Cat's husband, was also playing and was so engrossed in the game, he didn't even look up. He took these things very seriously. I stopped playing games with him after the great Christmas Pictionary Conflict a few years back. Don't ask, he's still upset about it.

Then came Carla and her husband, Paul. They were both twenty-six and had four-year-old twin girls, who gave me identical hugs and went back to their Barbies. My brother Rob and his girlfriend Michelle came up next. They were both so bright and full of life. My brother is the youngest in the family and was a bit of a... um, surprise. He and Michelle were finishing their last year of high school.

"Happy birthday, Rob." I hugged him warmly and then tossed him the DVD still in the bag.

"You didn't have time to wrap it?" my mother admonished as she chopped carrots.

"I've been busy, Mom," I said as gently as possible.

"Audition!" my brother shouted, apparently having opened the bag. "Oh my god, Phoenix, thank you! This looks awesome!" He hugged me again, a rare gift from a teenaged boy. He turned to Michelle. "Let's watch some before dinner." And they were off up the stairs to my brother's room.

My sister Cat, with baby Jenny on her hip, greeted me last.

"Hello, sweet pea." I call Jen sweet pea. Don't tell anybody, but she's my favourite.

"And hello to you too, Phoenix," Cat said dryly.

"Sorry, Cat." I smiled and gave her a quick half hug, avoiding knocking Jenny out of her arms. Jenny reached for me, and her mom passed her over. The two of us rubbed noses and giggled.

Yes, sometimes I giggle.

"I just haven't seen Jenny in so long."

"What are you talking about? You watched her last week."

"I did?" I asked, and then quickly remembered why it felt so long ago. You know, Time Travel. "Right, yeah, I did."

"Are you feeling okay, Phoenix?" my mom asked. "You sounded off this morning too."

"Yeah, sorry about that, Mom, I'd just overslept. I'm fine."

My mom responded by raising her eyebrows at me. As I bounced Jenny on my hip, she started to squirm.

"Ba ba ba!" She was pointing over my shoulder.

"What you looking at, sweet pea?"

I spun around and was greeted by our reflections. My breath stopped as I gazed into the big mirror that lived in my parents' kitchen. In the glass, the shimmery blue outline of my wings was startlingly clear. Jenny was pointing right at it. Cat came to stand beside us.

"There's nothing there, Jenny," she said to her child.

"Ba ba ba!"

Jenny was getting more agitated by the second, and I was frozen to the spot. How was this little baby seeing my Traveller reflection? I turned slightly, and the full girth of my wings was visible in the glass.

"Aaaah!" Jenny pushed away from me, crying.

"Sorry, Phoenix," Cat said as she plucked Jenny from my arms. "She must be tired. I'll go put her down for a bit."

"It's okay," I said in a faraway voice.

"She's usually so good with you," my mom mused. "Maybe she's coming down with something."

"Maybe."

I pulled my gaze from the glass and joined my mother at the kitchen counter. She was now chopping pearl onions; they were slipping around on the chopping board.

"That's a beautiful coat, honey. Is it new?"

"Yeah, I'm glad you like it."

"Where did you get it?"

As I was trying to think of an answer, an onion slipped from my mom's hand. The chopping knife sliced through her left index finger, which immediately started bleeding.

"Damn!" she dashed to the sink and began running cold water over the wound. "I will need a stitch!" She was scared but speaking low so as not to alarm the entire household.

"Let me look at it."

I took her hand and looked at the cut. It was deep and would require stitches, but I'd healed much worse.

"I think it just needs more cold water, Mom."

I placed her hand back under the tap and drew on my power. Subtly, I sent a thin line of energy down through my arms and into the wound. As my energy pulsed through my mother's flesh, the wound healed. The water grew hot as my energy leaked out into it.

"Ow!" My mom pulled her hand back from what she thought was a water tap gone haywire. "There's something wrong with that tap!" She grabbed some paper towel and wrapped it around her finger.

"It's fine, Mom." I turned off the tap. "How's your finger?"

"It's still bleeding, see…" She drew back the paper towel, which came away clean. "Oh, I guess it stopped."

"Are you sure? It was a nasty cut."

I stepped closer and examined the wound. The gash that had definitely needed stitches was now a tiny scratch. I hadn't had time to completely heal the cut, but this was better. She wouldn't think anything weird had happened.

"It's just a tiny scratch, you were worrying for nothing." My mom went back to the counter. "These onions won't chop themselves."

11

———

Dinner was relatively uneventful. As uneventful as dinner with nine adults, six children, two teenagers and an off-key chorus of happy birthday can be. Let's just say I'm glad I don't have to sit at the kids' table anymore.

We were all attempting to recline in our stiff back chairs, enjoying our full bellies, when I heard a tap at the dining room window. I turned to look out, but the brightly lit room had turned the windows into mirrors of blackness. All I could see was a slightly startled woman with wings, sitting in a room full of people who had eaten way too much cake. I turned back and told myself it was the wind.

Then the tap sounded again.

"Did you hear that?" my sister Lauren asked the group.

"You mean this?" my dad asked and then let out a massive belch.

"Oh, Michael!" my mother cried as a third tap sounded.

"There it is again!" Lauren said, rising from her seat. I hastily got to my feet.

"It's probably just Bonkers, I'll go let him in."

Bonkers, my parents' cat, and I didn't really get along, but I was glad to use him as cover now. I had a bad feeling about those sounds.

"I don't remember letting him out..." my mother said.

"What else could it be?" I said as happily as possible as I left the dining room.

I made my way down the hall that led from the kitchen to the back door. Once out of my family's field of vision, I dropped to a low run and switched out the hall light before I stood up and looked out on the yard. The dining room windows looked out onto the backyard, and this door opened to the same area. I could make out most of the yard in the light coming from the dining room. It spilled onto the lawn, bathing the first ten feet in warm yellow light.

I scanned the edges of the patch of light. A creature dashed through the field of light making me jump, but it was only Bonkers streaking towards the door. Something had spooked him. I opened the door as quietly as possible, and he rushed inside. Once over the threshold, he paused for a moment and looked surprised to find it was me who had opened the door. I shrugged in response, and he came forward and briefly rubbed his chin against my leg before running down the hall.

"Cool." Perhaps the cat and I had made peace. I returned to my surveillance of the backyard.

A shadowy figure moved at the edges of the field of light. It was small and low to the ground. Minion, I thought to myself. My suspicions were confirmed moments later when the creature took a step into the light, crawled up on the windowsill and tapped on the glass. I heard my sister say, "There it is again!" and I was out the door.

I drew forth my wings as I moved, shielding me from my family and exposing me to the minion tapping at my parents' window. It didn't hear me as I approached and I wasted no time in grabbing it by the neck and pulling it back into the shadows.

"Why are you here, little man?" I hissed in its ear. "I don't think you were invited to this party."

"Oh, you heard me," the creature said through a strangled throat. "Good. I wanted to talk to you for a moment."

"Then talk." I eased up my grip but did not let the minion go.

"Well, um, I've heard so much about you, I wanted to meet the creature behind the wings."

It stung a little that he said creature and not woman, or even human, but I guess those labels didn't really apply to me anymore.

"Wow," I replied, and with the Bounty out it had to be a lie. "You couldn't think of something better? Seriously?"

The minion sputtered a bunch of monosyllabic words in response.

"You must be one of Tog's friends. How's he doing?" I asked with a mocking tone.

"He's fine," said a second voice, strong and clear and very close. It was less phlegmy than the usual minion voice, and I spun towards the sound.

"Not alone, eh? Very smart," I said to the minion I had by the neck. I scanned the yard but could see nothing. "But where is your little friend?"

With a low hissing sound, something that looked like a mad hairless badger came running through the light. Before I could move, it slammed into my legs and drove me to the ground with my wings pinned under me. The minion I was holding seized the opportunity and kicked me in the chest.

It freaking hurt.

The two of them then went to work on me with their

teeny tiny fists. They were surprisingly strong, and I was glad that my family wouldn't be able to hear me yelping with pain. This tiny beat down went on for what felt like an eternity but was only about ten seconds. Seriously though, count to ten slowly. It's a long time. I was finally able to get my arms in front of me, and with a high-pitched scream, I force a shield of energy from my hands as my wings thrust me from the ground. The energy from my hands made a blast of clear white light, and when it subsided, I took a quick look through the dining room window. Everyone was laughing and talking, except baby Jenny who was standing on her mother's lap and pointing at me through the glass.

"How is this kid seeing me!?" I asked the night.

I didn't have time to dwell on that. The minions had recovered and were making a charge for me. One stood back and looked like he was preparing an energy ball and the other, the one I'd initially grabbed, was running at me with his fists raised. I took this all in within seconds and made my move.

I ran at the one charging me. At the last second I used a sharp extension of my wings to pivot and round-house kick him towards the other minion who, at that exact moment, had thrown the energy ball. This hit the first minion as he came barrelling towards him, and the two ended up tangled in what turned out to be an energy net.

"So that's your game," I said as I stalked towards them. "You think you're going to trap me. No dice, fellas."

Mr Energy Ball blanched at my approach and whispered a word that made the net disappear; he then took off at a run with the other minion on his heels.

"I don't think so." My wings flapped gently, lengthening my strides as I ran after them.

They were heading for the stream at the back of the

yard. It was beyond a thicket of trees and ran down into the neighbour's property. The Travel point must be on the other side of the water. I couldn't let them get away. They knew where my parents lived, and if they'd found Tog, they knew my neighbourhood too. If I didn't stop them, the whole Void would turn up for a slice of cake.

I chased them through the thicket, but they're minions, and no matter how well I knew that little patch of trees, their crazy hands and feet scramble would beat me every time on the rough terrain.

I saw the first minion leap into the air above the stream and disappear. The second had sprung into action when I grabbed his ankle.

I expected to feel chilly water on my skin as the minion and I plunged into the river. What I felt instead was my body being sucked into the fabric of Time as the bastard forced me to Travel.

12

———

I tried desperately to let go of that little jerk's ankle, and he tried desperately to shake me off, but no matter what either of us did, we were stuck together. And only one of us knew where we were going.

The lights of the Void portal flashed around us. Blue, green, pink, the occasional streak of red. They all passed by me as the minion screamed and thrashed. Realising that I wasn't getting rid of this guy, I took my free hand and grabbed for the minion's other leg. It took a few tries to raise my arm against the wind, but eventually, I got a hold of him with both hands. This left him with no choice but to fold against the wind and grab my hair, thus putting his minion crotch directly in my face.

Gross.

As quickly as we entered the portal, we were out. We hit what felt like wood, but it bent considerably beneath us, and we began the dance of trying to shake off the other without losing our grip on our opponent. For the minion in front of me, this meant trying to grab my neck. I kept one hand clamped on his ankle and used the other to push him off, but he still had one hand wrapped up in my hair, and it hurt like hell.

I had completely forgotten about my powers, but my body hadn't and when the jerk tried to bite my face it responded. A blast of dark green energy, strong, protective and angry, ripped from my mouth and threw the minion off me and into the air.

As the creature cleared my face, I took in two things simultaneously; we were on a bridge, and the minion was going over the side.

Without thinking, I leapt over the side of the bridge, tucking and rolling as I sailed through the air, my wings tight to my back. I saw the minion beneath me and reached out a hand, catching him once again by the ankle, my wings flapping in a hard reverse as we hovered just inches from the ground. The minion's face touched the dirt, and he whimpered. Dangling him by the ankle, I flew back up to the bridge.

As I did, I took in my surrounding. We were in an ancient forest. We also had to be somewhere on the north-west coastline because as far as I could see every tree in this forest was a giant redwood.

The trees were widely spaced, and although it wasn't super comfortable, I could fly in a muscled sort of way between them. I found the bridge I had jumped from and then followed it along through the trees looking for the other minion.

"Where's your friend, big boy?" I asked the minion.

"Oh, he'll be long gone now." The minion chuckled, hacking up a big wad of phlegm that he allowed to fall to the forest floor.

"Gross!" I shook the minion to make sure his excretions didn't get on me.

"The great warrior is afraid of a little spit? That is hilarious," the minion laughed again, so I dropped him.

He screamed, and I let him fall five or six feet before I swooped down and caught him.

"Now who's scared?" I asked mildly as I flew back up to the maze of rope bridges.

They seemed to go on forever; wide, perfectly spaced pieces of wood lashed together with thick rope and draped from tree to tree. It would have taken years to create such a system, and how the hell would you get up here in the first place?

"What is this place?"

The minion was still recovering from his fright, and it took him a few seconds to answer.

"It's a secret."

This time I tossed him up into the air.

He screamed again as he sailed in a beautiful high arch over the bridge beside us. I landed on the bridge as he flew over the opposite side and reached out, snatched him from the air, then tossed him onto the bridge. He landed on his stomach with a grunt. My wings stretched to stabilize me as I used the toe of my boot to roll him onto his back. I placed my boot squarely on his chest, pinning him.

"All right, I've had enough of your shit. You and your buddies have followed me, threatened my family and punched me far more than I would deem acceptable. I've kicked your ass a couple times now, and I'm willing to do it again if you continue to piss me off. So this is what's going to happen; I will let you sit up, and you will answer my questions." I leant into my leg, making him gasp. "And if you try to screw with me, I am going punt you off this bridge. Understand?"

The minion nodded.

"Good boy."

I slowly lifted my boot from the tiny creature's chest and took a small step back. At first, he didn't move, just lay there looking at me with a wary gaze, then ever so slowly, like he was moving a single vertebra at a time, he rolled up through his spine to a seated position. It was a move any Pilates instructor would be proud of.

"Impressive."

He smiled a little self-indulgently and then settled himself into a cross-legged position. With a good deal less grace, I held on to the ropes and lowered myself onto the bridge, mirroring him.

"The rumour is true," the minion said.

"What rumour?"

"That you've changed."

"Yeah, I get that a lot."

I was really getting tired of hearing that. What did these creatures expect? I'd lost all my memories of the Void when I'd been reborn as a human, and I'd had to fight most of these jerks to get my wings back. Stuff like that changes a person.

"What's your name?" The question surprised him.

"You wish to know my name? Why?"

"Because I'm talking to you," I said dryly. "Look, this will go a lot faster if you don't question every question."

"True. Okeg, I am called Okeg."

"Okay, Okeg. Second question; did Tog tell you where to find me?"

"Oh, poor Tog," the minion laughed, hacked up something heavy and spat it off the side of the bridge. "You did a real number on him. It took us hours to find him, and when he got out of the box, the newspaper had stained his forehead. Everyone kept asking him 'what's the headline!'"

He laughed again, and I had to fight from joining him.

"Okay, that's pretty funny," I smiled, and Okeg stopped laughing and stared at me. "What?"

"You are pretty for a humanoid."

"Thanks." I don't think I could have added more sarcasm to the word if I'd tried.

"And for all your angry words, your energy is clean and kind. I can see that now as we sit here." He regarded me. "Who would put a Bounty on your head?"

"So you don't know?"

"I do not."

"Greldrom sent you all after me with no explanation?"

"He is our leader; he need not explain."

There was something about the way Okeg said those words that lead me to believe he was monumentally unhappy with the situation.

"And was Tog telling me the truth, the person who brings me to Greldrom gets a share of my power?"

"That is what we have been told."

"I will assume that appeals to you since you tracked me down."

He nodded.

"Okay, back to my first question, where are we?" I flared my wings. "And don't give me that secret shit."

"We are in a minion stronghold."

"What!?" I scrambled to my feet. Okeg sat there serenely.

"Yes, Phoenix, this is a place where minions gather. In fact, if you listen closely you can hear hundreds of my brothers approaching."

"No..."

I breathed the word as my ears strained against the sounds of the forest. I could indeed hear a multitude of tiny hands and feet slapping against wood. And the sound was growing louder. The bridge swayed subtly. Panic nibbled at me, I looked left and right, trying to see my attackers approach.

"There is no escape, Phoenix," Okeg was slowly getting to his feet. "Your pretty face will twist in pain as I take my share of your power." He was speaking so quietly, it made the sound of approaching minions even more frightening. His voice lowered to a whisper, "We will tear you apart."

At that moment hundreds of minions broke like a wave over the bridge in front of me. The bridge shook violently with their weight. I screamed. Then I ran.

Panic took over as I saw more minions approaching from the many bridges on either side of me. I could feel the minions at my back getting closer. I ran and screamed and ran, my lungs ripping as the air pumped in and out of me. My head was full of blind panic and fear. My wings shook and flashes of the terrible day when they were torn from my body raced through my mind, filling my centre with cold icy terror.

I ran until I found myself on a platform, a junction between many bridges. I spun around and found minions surrounded me. They raced towards me from every angle. I had nowhere to turn.

I stood silent with fear as they broke onto the platform and cascaded over me. It was a wave of tiny hands and teeth pinching and pulling at my body. I pulled myself into a ball at the base of the pile as images of my first attack moved like a strobe light through my body. I heard a minion scream "Wings!" It pulled me from the flashback and snapped me into reality, lighting a fuse of rage in my belly. It filled me with deep blood red power that exploded from my body like a land mine. Every minion touching me was thrown violently back, taking his brothers with him as they screamed in pain. I looked at their flesh; it was burned where my power had touched it.

My power continued outward, creating a shield of fire around me. The minions it touched writhed in pain, and the others scrambled back, screaming as my shield caught them, burning where it touched. I stood calmly within the flaming orb.

A voice shouted above the din of screaming minions and the stench of burning flesh.

"Let me through, let me through!"

Okeg broke through the crowd and froze, taking in the carnage. I called to him from within my burning shield.

"You will never taste my power, Okeg. None of you will." I laughed at the fear on his face. "Tell Greldrom, I am coming for him."

And then I Travelled.

13

———

I landed on my hands and knees on the bank of the stream. I dug my fingers into the mud and let out a guttural yell of rage.

"Damn it!" I shouted and pulled my hands back from the filth. "Damn it! Damn it! Damn it!"

How could I let the minions get the drop on me like that? Why am I always so trusting? I had no idea what world I was in and yet I sat down with Okeg like we were old friends.

And the pain, so much pain, the fear and loss had come rushing back. It felt like I was right back there in the Void, pinned down and assaulted yet again. The little hands, then and now felt like a thousand blades slicing at my skin. I yelled again and pounded my fists into the ground. I would not let those bastards win by succumbing to the anxiety that was threatening my bones. I would get up and find Big G and put an end to this. He might not have called the Bounty, but he knew who did. And he would tell me.

"Phoenix!?"

My mother.

Crap.

She had followed me into the woods. At first, I stayed where I was, thinking she couldn't see me with my wings exposed, then I realised that during my raging I had retracted them. I was now entirely visible as I threw a tantrum in the mud.

A flashlight beam cut through the trees.

Double crap.

I got to my feet and scrambled to some bushes a few feet away and wiped the mud from my hands on the branches. I tried to clean up the rest of me; the coat seemed miraculously clean, but my pants and boots were soaked.

"Phoenix, are you down here?"

"I'm here, Mom." I made my way up the slope towards her, furiously thinking of a way to explain my appearance. "Sorry, I couldn't find Bonkers."

"He's in the house, sweetheart."

"Oh, I thought I heard him down here." Her flashlight beam hit me, burning my eyes. "Mom!"

"Phoenix! What happened to you?" Her voice was practically a screech as she took in my appearance.

"Well, I fell in the stream, didn't I?" Yeah, fell in the stream, that'll work. Thanks, brain.

"What were you doing down there?"

"Looking for Bonkers."

"But he's in the house!"

This was getting very circular.

"Yes, Mom, you said, but I didn't know that or I wouldn't have come down here."

"Your boots are ruined."

They really were, as was my patience. I was cold and wet and had a big bad creature to hunt down. I needed to get out of here.

"Yes, Mother, I am aware of that."

"Well," she was getting pissy now, too. "You better come inside and get out of those clothes."

We were almost at the house, and she strode past me towards the door.

"No, Mom." She spun on her heel.

"What do you mean no?"

This could get bad, I needed to do some placating and fast. Creature from another world scared of her mommy.

"Well, mom, look at me. I'm a mess, I'll scare the kids. Let me just head home and get changed. I'll call Rob tomorrow and make my apologies."

She looked unconvinced. Time to bring out the big guns.

"Besides," I paused for effect, "I'll ruin your floors."

That did the trick.

"Yes, dear, you're probably right. Just run around the side of the house, I'll say your goodbyes." She leant forward and, careful to not touch my clothes, kissed me on my cheek. "Be good."

"I always am."

She headed inside; I walked slowly until I knew she was behind a locked door and then ran to my car. The engine was running, and the door was open by the time I reached the vehicle. I paused before getting in and turned to the house; I needed to do something to protect my family until this was all over.

I called forth my power. It cracked like a whip in my belly and filled me instantly with a warm green energy.

"Woah," I breathed, watching the green energy drip from fingertips. Instead of dropping to the ground, it floated towards the house.

"Cool!"

I focused and threw my hands towards the house. I

swiped at the air like a painter and watched as vast swathes of green energy flew towards the house, coating it in a glowing protective shell.

Once the entire house was covered, I got in my car. It immediately started moving. I grabbed the wheel and forced a deep breath in and out of my lungs.

"Easy, Phoenix, take it easy."

The car slowed down, responding to my new calm. I was a little jumpy after the events of the evening. I needed someone to talk to; the car would have to do.

"There is no way I'm going back to the city tonight. I need a place to stash you for a little while."

An image of an empty parking lot and a small, lonely building flashed through my mind.

"The train station, excellent idea."

Honestly, I don't know if it was mine or the car's.

14

———

I drove slowly through the train station parking lot. It was late, and the lot was deserted. I pulled around behind the ticket booth and parked a few rows back. Hopefully, any passersby would just think I'd missed my train home and leave the car alone.

I got out of the car. Somewhere in the dark, a bird cried out, and I jumped, whacking my head on the doorjamb.

"Shit!" I rubbed my head with my hand and felt dried mud flake off. "Gross, I need a shower," I sighed heavily. "A soft bed and some powerful arms to carry me there." A happy thought filled me from the tips of my toes to the top of my bruised head. "Maybe Archer is back."

This put a spring in my step, and I crossed the parking lot, enjoying myself as I skipped my way between the pools of light that dotted the asphalt. There were some trees at the edges of the lot, and I stood in their shadows, took a deep breath and made a call of power to Travel home.

Nothing happened.

Refusing to panic, I took a deep breath and, even though I was hoping to avoid doing it here, called forth my wings.

They spread out behind me, and as my power rose, I called them to Travel.

Again, nothing happened.

Now I was panicking. Big time. Big. Panic. Time.

I heard someone hyperventilating. I spun around looking for the source of the sound and realised it was me. I forced myself to stop moving. It was a struggle; everything in me was screaming I was trapped. It was too much after the minion attack. I fell to my knees, put my head between them and wrapped my wings around myself like a cocoon.

I forced a breath deep into my lungs, feeling my rib cage move and my wings shift in sympathy. I let it out as slowly and completely as I could and then inhaled again, pushing the air deeper this time. My shoulders loosened, and my mind stilled. The third breath came more easily, and soon I was breathing deeply and calmly.

Keeping my eyes closed, I sat up slowly and shifted into a cross-legged position. I straightened my spine and focused on Travel. I pictured the tunnel of Time and Space that I would move through, and the place outside my gates where I would land. I relived it over and over in my mind: the way the wind would whip against me, the feel of the hard earth beneath my feet as I landed, the smell of the trees in the air. When the sensations became second nature to my mind, I opened my eyes.

I was still looking out on the deserted parking lot, but something in the distance caught my eye. Hovering over the tracks was a shimmery ball of energy. It moved and twisted like a cluster of fireflies, dancing and undulating in the air directly over the tracks.

A swoop of my wings brought me to my feet, and I started across the pavement towards the light. Another swoop of wings and I'd easily vaulted over the high barricade between the parking lot and the tracks.

I looked up at the undulating ball of silvery energy and reached out a finger to touch it. Even stretched out at my considerable height, I still couldn't quite reach it. I stepped up onto the track and reached up. My finger touched just a single moat of light and an image of the Time Tunnel flared in my mind as energy shot through my body, throwing me to the ground.

"Wow," I said to myself. "I guess that's the portal."

The ground rumbled beneath me. It was subtle at first, but soon every inch of me was shaking, I struggled to my feet as a deep whistle sounded.

A train was coming.

"Shit!" I'd been saying that far too much lately.

I looked down the tracks, and the train was almost on me.

"How can something that big sneak up on me?" I asked no one in particular.

I would have to jump for it.

With no time to lose, I took a few steps back and ran towards the portal. I stepped onto the rail for a boost, but it was shaking so hard that what was supposed to be a clean dive became a jumbled bunch of limbs that rushed painfully into the ball of light.

"At least I'm heading home," I grunted as worlds flashed by.

15

———————

I t occurred to me as I Travelled, that perhaps, until now, I had just been lucky with finding spots to Travel from. Maybe what I saw at the train station was actually the way it worked all the time, I'd just never had to be aware of it before. This knowledge would hopefully keep me from panicking next time I couldn't instantly hit a portal.

I landed on my feet in the forest that surrounded my home.

My home.

After the events of the day, it felt more like my true home than ever before. My apartment was no longer safe and, last time I checked, was covered in goo. And I couldn't go to my parents' home because it brought creatures to their doorstep. This compound in the middle of this beautiful, breezy forest was my sanctuary, and I had the gargoyles to prove it.

"You're back! You're back!"

Brog was standing on the tips of his toes, his little stone

wings flapping, as he vigorously waved to me. Grog sat calmly, a welcoming smile on his face.

"Welcome home, my lady."

"Hi, guys."

They gasped. I looked down at my muck-covered body. Why do I always seem to end up so dirty?

"It's okay, guys," I held my hands up, and they closed their little mouths. "I'm not hurt, just dirty. Nothing a shower and a change of clothes can't fix."

"That's a relief," Brog beamed at me. Grog was not so easily convinced.

"And how did you get so dirty, lady?" He spoke like he was addressing a queen, a tremendous feat when I looked like the rat I'd punted down the alley a few hours ago.

"Well, I fell in a stream, but the real problem was the unexpected trip to the minion stronghold..." I had intended to continue, but both gargoyles cried out.

"What! How did you end up there?" Grog said, his stony brows rose in a look of shock.

"That's a bad, bad place," Brog had teared up, little tiny pebbles dribbled from the corners of his eyes.

"I know that now." I patted Brog on the head and sat down beside him on the stone platform. He wriggled in close beside me. It could feel his stony body move as he breathed.

"Bad place," he whispered, closed his eyes and immediately began to snore.

"So how did you get there, lady?" Grog asked again, sitting down across from me.

"I was tricked," I stroked Brog's back; it was like petting a cement cat. "Some minions tracked me to my parents' house, and when I tried to catch them, they jumped into a portal. I got stuck to one of them and dragged to their destination."

"The underground caves?" Grog asked.

"Underground caves?"

"Ah, so they took you to the City in the Trees," Grog looked thoughtfully into the middle distance. "You were lucky; it is a far less dangerous place as these things go." He looked at me with his slate eyes. "You must never go to the caves, my lady. Never. Down in their warren, they will toy with you and tear you apart, piece by piece." He shuddered. "I met a gargoyle who had been dragged down there as a gift for their leader..."

"Big G," I said.

"Big G?"

"Greldrom."

"Oh," a slight smile crept across his face, "I like it." He continued, "This gargoyle told me terrible things about what goes on there," I opened my mouth to ask. "Things I will not repeat to a lady." I opened my mouth again. "No matter how much she asks me. He eventually escaped by sneaking up to the surface through an underground stream. He said it was the scariest place he had ever been." Grog shuddered.

"Where is it?"

Moving surprisingly quickly for a hunk of stone, Grog leapt across the stoop and landed on the ledge beside me. He grabbed my shoulder and twisted me to face him. Brog woke with a start and scrambled away from me.

"You must never, never go there, Phoenix!" He shook me. "Never! They will peel the flesh from your skin and smoke it while you watch. They will eat you slowly, using their magic to keep you alive so you can scream with every bite." Pebbles fell freely from his eyes. They pinged against the ground, making a musical sound. "Greldrom will pluck every feather from your wings and keep you chained to his throne." Brog started to cry. It sounded like gravel being poured onto tiles. "Please promise us you will never go there!" Grog panted.

"Come here." I opened my arms, and they crawled into my lap. They were heavy, really heavy. I had to make this quick or risk losing feeling in my legs. I hugged them tightly. "I promise you, I will never go to the minion city in the caves."

I meant every word, yet something deep in the back of my consciousness disagreed. Some small part of me wondered if Sid was there.

"Thank you, lady," Grog sniffed, stones rattled inside his head. "Please forgive my..."

"Not necessary, Grog."

He smiled wearily and crawled back to his spot. I peeled Brog away from my chest and looked him in the eyes. Black orbs dribbling grey pebbles. I wiped them away and patted him on his chipped stone skull.

"It's okay, Brog. I'll stay safe." He looked tired. "Why don't you go back to sleep?"

"Yes, lady." He crawled to the end of the platform and curled into a little stone ball.

I got to my feet. I needed a shower and maybe even a catnap. This day was proving long and extremely stressful, but first I had one more question for Grog. One I was pretty sure I knew the answer to.

"Has Archer stopped by?"

Grog only shook his head and then took up his position at the end of his platform.

16

I messed with the faucet until I had the right temperature, just this side of scalding, and then stepped back to let it do its work filling the bathtub. Yes, a shower would be faster, but my legs ached, and besides getting clean I needed to sit down.

My beautiful coat already draped across my bed, it seemed to miraculously repel dirt; I sat down on the padded bench in the middle of the spacious bathroom that adjoined my bedroom and peeled my boots from my feet. I tossed them near the door where they landed with a squelch.

Yep, ruined.

I stood and reached back to unsnap the straps that entwined my body. With the straps free, the garment slipped easily around my wings and from my torso. From the waist down was another matter; I was caked in mud and muck. It was like getting a wetsuit off, and as enormous chunks of dirt fell to the floor, I was glad it was made of marble.

With the bathtub still filling, it's a full-on soaker tub, almost a small pool, really, I went to the vanity and selected a silver comb and some delicious soaps and shampoos. I opened one bottle and took a deep sniff. Mint, lavender and something lovely yet unidentifiable met my senses. In my former life, I had great taste in toiletries.

The tub was almost full, and I slipped into the water as the faucet raged on. I let my body disappear completely bellow the water's surface, my wings splaying out beneath me. Once submerged I lay still and let the water support my weight. The tub was big enough that I could almost stretch out to my full height and my wings could open slightly. I opened my eyes and looked up through the crystal clear water to the sparkling chandelier that hung above the tub. It winked at me and even with the Bounty on my head; I felt very, very lucky.

I broke the surface and took a deep breath of the steamy air around me. I turned off the tap. Selecting a light blue concoction, I started the lengthy process of shampooing, conditioning and detangling my hair. I love having long hair, but there are times, like after a fight, that I consider buzzing it all off. Tangles are serious bitches.

The first stage of hair cleaning complete, I let the shampoo soak in and reached for a big sponge. Now, this is not your ordinary pink, plastic, man-made sponge, this is a colossal piece of dried botanical wonderfulness that cleans better than anything I'd ever used. I squirted some sweet smelling green goop on it and then stood up so I could scrub my legs. The sponge made quick work of the job, and I relished the soft tinkling sound that filled the air as tiny drops of water beaded on my wings and fell into the tub.

I slipped under the water again and ran my hands over my body and through my hair, rinsing myself clean. Then I went for the conditioner and the comb and set about the business of detangling. The big comb was obviously an antique, there was a detailed scrolling design of vines and flowers along the handle, and the silver had a lustre to it that only time can provide. I was careful not to let it fall in the tub, and once my hair was thoroughly combed I rinsed the comb under the tap and laid it in the sun to dry off. I know it's only a comb, but I felt a deep affinity with it. Which is also strange, yes, but what about my life isn't?

I submerged for a third time and ran my fingers through my hair until I was sure the conditioner had left its surface. Now squeaky clean, I hit a button that started the tub's jets and lay back to enjoy the swirling water. All the various soaps in the water foamed, and the combined scents were ultra-relaxing.

My eyelids drooped, and I let them, succumbing to sleep right there in the swirling warmth.

17

The current was strong, but I was stronger. My arms cut through the salty water like blades and I dropped and shifted with the waves, evading every current that sought to own me. My wings were like two dorsal fins at my back, and as a massive wave made to crest over me, they slammed themselves wide against it, throwing me into the air where I somersaulted and then dove into the breach.

My wings flattened against my body, and I plunged deeper and deeper. The pressure in my lungs growing as the water pressed in around them.

How deep could I go? How far could I push myself? Nothing mattered. Not the pain in my lungs or the tunnelling of my vision or the heat building in my face and hands. Nothing. I would push myself into oblivion and then there would be darkness.

Cold hands suctioned to me like a squid, grabbing my shoulder and pulling me back. I struggled against them, but I was losing strength. Blackness was licking blissfully at my eyes. I would be gone before they could pull me to the surface. Gone. Nothing.

The hands shifted, I felt a body between my wings as arms wrapped around my shoulders. Powerful legs kicked beside me. Faster and faster we rose. I cried out. Begging my captor to let me be. To let me drift. Salt touched my tongue. Maybe they were too late.

Suddenly air filled my lungs. My body gulped it down as my mind reeled. My vision returned as a familiar face formed before me. We bobbed up and down with the waves.

"Don't you ever, ever do that again!"

Hmm, I thought, Noiryn is yelling at me. Then everything went black once more.

18

I screamed as I nearly sprang from the tub. Icy water splashed everywhere as my wings spread violently. I struggled in the water, slipping on the soapy bottom of the bath as my brain and body tried to find each other. I tumbled from the tub, my wings the only thing sparing me from cracking my head on the marble. I crawled on hands and knees to the bench and leant against it, pulling my robe over me with shaking hands. I forced my breathing to slow and my mind to focus.

"It was only a dream. Only a dream," I intoned.

But was it? It had felt very real; even now I could taste salt on my tongue. Since we had reunited, my wings had been showing me snippets of my past. What if this was one of those visions? What if I had actually tried to swim to the bottom of the ocean?

"No, Phoenix," I said to myself, "it was a dream. You fell asleep in the tub, you probably swallowed some water, and your brain freaked out trying to wake you." I wiped the tears from my eyes. "That's all."

I was having a full on conversation with myself. And we

disagreed. The realization of this made me laugh, and the action made the deep core of my power tingle with warmth. I let the laughter grow, and the warmth in me filled my torso and cascaded through my body. I felt better. I felt hungry.

"We need to eat!" I told myself with a chuckle.

I rose to my feet and headed to the kitchen.

19

Once fed and clothed, I sat by the fire and plotted my next few moves. I definitely needed to go see Benyst and Noiryn again before I looked for Greldrom, and I definitely need to find Archer before I did that. Once I'd found Archer, and bitch slapped Big G a few dozen times, I needed to locate the asshole who put this Bounty on my head and make them remove it. With force, if necessary. Everything started with a trip to the jungle, but first I needed some supplies. Time to go to the war room.

Okay, it isn't technically a war room. There aren't vast banks of computers and giant screens and lots of men in dishevelled suits yelling at each other, but there are a lot of very cool Traveller warrior type things.

I had discovered the room on my second day back in the house. I was exploring the greenhouse when I noticed a door hidden behind some vines. It opened at my touch to reveal a room full of interesting things. Standing in the middle of the room now, in a jumpsuit made of thick stretch cotton and a pair of far more rugged boots, I surveyed my options.

There was a wall of satchels and harnesses, each custom designed to hold one of the weapons on the opposite wall. Weapons might be too strong a word. It was mainly a wall of wooden staffs and short pipes. When I'd first found the space, I wondered why a Traveller would need weapons when they held so much personal power. I had since been physically overpowered enough times to know it was nice to have a backup.

I had added the broken half of the bat I'd pulled from Archer's belly to the wall, and its bright blue paint stood out amongst the dull wood and muted metal of the various staffs and whacking type items. I ran my fingers over the bat, tracing over the bits of Archer's blood that had dried on the shattered end. Archer. Where could he be? Why had I never insisted he showed me where his home was? I was scared, and I could really use his support. I didn't want to do this alone, but I would if I had to. I looked at the destroyed bat. Even whole it would no longer be an adequate defence for the world I lived in. It felt bittersweet to remember a simpler time when finding my wings was all I had to worry about.

A glint of silver caught my eye.

I looked directly at where I had seen the spark but saw nothing that might cause the shimmer. I stepped back from the wall and surveyed the expanse but could see no metal bright enough to catch my eye.

Using my brain box, I stepped up to the wall and waited for the glint to shine again.

Nothing.

I sighed and looked at the bat. The Archer's silver blood was soaked into the wood, it looked like mercury. I reached out and touched it, feeling the texture of splinters and the traces of Archer's energy that had fused to them.

"Archer," I whispered.

The glint of silver sparked again. I focused on the blood, wood and love before me.

"Archer," I said more forcefully.

The silver shone again, longer this time, but still, it faded before I could move. Pulling on the coil of energy in my belly, I drew my love's name from the centre of myself. I felt power course through my wings.

"Archer!"

With a shout of power, a silver light blazed in the room. It shone like ice and sun. I stood back from the wall to track it. There, near the bottom of the wall, was the source. I moved closer, and the light dimmed, revealing its shape to me.

It was a sword.

An elegant silver sword the length of my arm. I reached for the hilt, and my hand met jewels. I pulled it from the wall to find it was lightweight yet firm as stone, straight as an arrow. "Archer," I whispered to the sword. An engraving appeared on the shaft, and I lifted it to my eyes to read the word. Phoenix. It was a gift from him; I knew it in my bones.

"Thank you," I spoke to him, hoping the sentiment would find him.

I swung the sword a few times. The metal felt like a natural extension of my body. Energy prickled my hands as I held the blade and I knew it would happily travel down the shaft if called. I smiled.

"Now to find your holster."

The words had barely left my mouth when the sound of leather hitting the floor filled my ears. I turned to find a bundle of grey leather lying on the floor. Placing the sword on a small table at the end of the room, I scooped the leather pile up off the floor.

It was the sheath for the sword. The long tube inlaid

with mother of pearl was the exact size and shape of the blade. The straps, however, were longer than I would have expected for a sheath worn at the waist and it took me several hilarious attempts to lash it around me before I realised where it was meant to be worn.

The straps entwined the base of my wings and around my shoulders, thus placing the blade at a slight angle along my spine. This meant I would draw the blade by reaching over my right shoulder and pulling it out and down in an arch to the left of my body.

With the harness in place, I lifted the blade and made to put it in the sheath. The blade was light enough that I could lift it easily with my right hand, which was good because my left hand was trying valiantly to hold my hair out of the way. I poised the blade above what I hoped, since I couldn't see behind me, was the mouth of the sheath.

"Oh, please don't cut off my hair."

The blade took over, sliding into the sheath with ease. I felt it move against my hair and yet it didn't cut a single strand. Like Noiryn's lamp and Benyst's string, it heard my request and made it happen. This was a great present.

Dressed for adventure, I walked back through the greenhouse to the front hall. I grabbed my starry coat from the bannister and slipped into it. With my hair draped over the jacket's collar, it completely hid the sword. It still felt strange to leave the house without a purse, but with power at my fingertips, there was no need for kleenex and a driver's license.

I stepped quietly out the front door, hoping that the gargoyles were asleep. They were, and I tip-toed quickly past them. I didn't want to answer any awkward questions about where I was going, and I really didn't want to lie to them. Yes, I said I wouldn't go to the city in the caves, and I honestly hoped I'd never have to see the inside of that hell-hole, but if that's where my journey took me, well, that's where I would go.

But first I needed to check in with my jungle friends.

20

———

I landed in the circle of torches; they blazed brightly against the inky sky. It always seemed to be night in Benyst's world. I paused for a moment, waiting for the inevitable squeal from Noiryn as she dashed around the hut to meet me, but all was silent in the clearing. I rolled my shoulders, feeling the sword move against my back, and walked towards the hut.

All the curtains were drawn, and as I walked around to the front of the hut, I discovered the curtain that acted as a door was also pulled tight. Weird. The only time I'd ever seen a curtain closed was when I took a shower out back. Usually, everything was left open so the rare jungle breeze could flow through. I stepped back from the door and called out.

"Benyst?"

I heard a feminine gasp, a thud, and a deep grunt. So they were here. Things seemed to be getting mighty interesting between these two.

"Just a second, just a second!" Benyst's deep voice

sounded, it felt less gravelly than before. An enormous grin spread across my face.

"Take your time," I retorted.

"Well, maybe you should announce yourself next time," Benyst called back.

The curtain twitched as I prepared my witty response, but the words died in my throat as Benyst stepped out into the torchlight.

His tumours were gone.

All of them. Gone. In their place was a face more handsome than any I'd seen in a long time. My jaw hit the floor. Benyst looked like he'd stepped out of a romance novel. Powerful square jaw, thick neck, soft lips and piercing blue eyes. He was standing taller too; I had never noticed how broad his shoulders were. He moved like a king as he pushed the curtain aside and tied it back. He gave Archer a run for his money.

"Are you going to just stand there staring?"

I continued to stare. It was remarkable, Benyst's skin was smooth and whole, his eyes clear, his hair lay flat against his skull.

"You're blowing my mind right now."

He smiled and; I didn't think it was possible, but my jaw dropped further.

"Holy shit," I whispered.

"It's amazing, isn't it?" Noiryn slipped by him and ran to my side, grabbing my hand. "They were getting better and better, then all of a sudden, gone!" She beamed at him.

"Not all of a sudden, Noi."

He reached out a hand for her and she went to him. He kissed her deeply, and I watched shamelessly. They were a hot couple. They broke from their kiss and smiled at each other.

"Now the outside matches the inside," I said.

"Exactly!" Benyst exclaimed. "You always were a smart one, Phoenix. My insides and my outsides match. That's how my people are. For the first time in a long time, I'm happy."

"That's wonderful, guys." And it was. But for some reason Noiryn was frowning. "What's up, Noiryn?"

"Why are you carrying a sword?"

Shit.

"Damn. You can see it?" I asked, trying to look over my shoulder. I'll never learn.

"What sword?" Benyst asked, his tone growing concerned.

"The one she is hiding at her back."

Damn, she's perceptive.

"Let me see it."

I drew the blade from its sheath; it slid through my hair like silk. I stepped forward and twisted the sword, so the hilt was within Benyst's reach. He took the blade from me and walked away. As Noiryn and I watched, he tested the sword, swinging it back and forth, parrying and jabbing occasionally. Noiryn and I shared a glance; apparently, we were both shocked by his prowess with a blade. Satisfied he had inspected in thoroughly, he handed the sword back to me. I offered it to Noiryn, and she shook her head no. As I put the blade away, Benyst spoke.

"That is a remarkable blade. Where did you get it?"

"Archer gave it to me." The blade became momentarily hot in my hand but slid home without incident.

"A powerful gift."

"But why are you carrying it?" Noiryn asked again. I sighed. They weren't going to like this.

"Because..." I kicked at the dirt at my feet and then,

mustering the strength, looked her in the eyes. "Because I'm going after Greldrom."

Their reactions were as I expected. A lot of yelling, a few tears, and some heavy foot stomping as I was told over and over how terrible my idea was. When they both took a breath, I slipped into the silence.

"I agree with you. It is a stupid idea, one that's guaranteed to backfire. However, it's the only way. Greldrom has sent every minion in the Void after me. They've almost caught me twice. He may not have put the Bounty on my head, but he's determined to collect it. I need to get to the bottom of this, all of it, and every time I think it through it all leads back to Big G himself."

"Big G?" Benyst whispered the question.

"Greldrom, Big G is just easier."

"I like it," he chuckled. Noiryn slapped his arm.

"I need to find him, kick his ass and make him take me to whoever has put this Bounty on my head. Then I'm going to kick their ass and make them call everything off."

"So why the sword?" Noiryn asked, again.

I knew what she was really asking. A sword is a lethal weapon; you don't take it out just to scare people. Noiryn wanted to know if I was prepared to use it. And, well, I wasn't sure yet, but in the game of them or me, I knew whose side I was on.

"Things might get heavy."

She looked away, but that third eye stayed locked on me. It was unnerving, but I didn't flinch.

"First, I need to find Archer. Any leads?"

"Nothing concrete," Benyst replied. "But we heard that Silverwood has been to his place. He may tell you where it is if he's actually been there."

"It's a start. How do I get to Silverwood?"

"Ah," Benyst dragged out the word. "That's the problem. We know approximately where he is, but once you're there, you'll have to do some serious legwork."

"Such as?" I asked suspiciously.

"Hiking. He's somewhere near Deer Cave in old time Borneo."

"What do you mean, old time Borneo?"

"Well, that's what your time calls it." Something moved in his cheek, like a bug under the skin, and was gone.

"Well, Borneo is a big place and 'old time,'" I made angry bunny ears, also known as air quotes, with my fingers, "isn't very specific. How am I supposed to find Silverwood?"

"All right, now just calm down," Benyst said.

Never tell me to calm down. Never. It just makes me, as it does most women, go silent and visualize the ways in which I will exact my revenge when you least expect it. Noiryn knew this and quietly said Benyst's name. He took a deep breath, rolled his sizeable shoulders and continued.

"The image has been given to me, I may not be able to articulate the time he is in, but I can take you there."

"What do you mean 'the image has been given to you'?"

Before he could explain, Noiryn jumped in.

"Because we operate outside of Time, directions can be difficult, so we take a moment to place an image of the location in the other's heart. When tapped, this image will take you to the place and time intended by the other Traveller."

"Sounds reasonable. So who gave you the image, Benyst? I thought you didn't go out much."

"I still have a few friends on the outside."

He said it without a trace of mirth and did not elaborate. I let the matter drop. He was already heading to the clearing.

"Let's go."

"Sure," I said to his back as I made to follow.

When Noiryn made no move to join us, I turned to her.

"You're not coming?"

"No. I'll wait here."

I prepared myself for the usual robust goodbye, but it didn't come.

"Well... bye."

I moved to hug her. She responded physically, but her heart was nowhere near the embrace. "Noiryn, have I done something wrong?"

She laughed bitterly.

"I guess sometimes I miss the old you."

Without another word, she went into the hut.

21

Man, I hate co-Travelling. The trip through the portal with Benyst was a real hack job. The last time I'd Travelled with him I'd had one wing and no idea what was going on. That was the Phoenix he'd expected on this journey, so he flooded me with power as he gripped my arms. I spent the entire trip stuck in a circuit of his energy with his hot breath on my face. It was uncomfortable.

We landed flat out on the spongy ground front to front with, thankfully, me on top. The sword would not have felt good jammed into my back. Both of us tried simultaneously to get away from the other, causing a lot of wriggling. I was about to complain when I looked into Benyst's face. His devastatingly handsome face. I stopped moving. He stopped moving. We stared at each other. One heartbeat. Two heartbeats. Something inside me woke up. Benyst shifted against me as his hand lightly brushed my thigh, and that thing in me tingled.

"Oh, this is bad. Very bad." The words were coming out of my mouth, but my body remained where it was.

"Yes, yes, it is." His voice was husky and low. My toes curled ever so slightly. He cleared his throat. "Mainly because you wouldn't have lingered this long if I was still disfigured."

His words slapped me across the face. With a quick flap of my wings, I was standing, looking down at him.

"Wow," I shook my head. "Thanks for the ride." I turned on my heel and marched away from him. He didn't call my name, didn't come after me, and when I turned back, he was gone. "Well, that's two friendships I've screwed up today. Excellent work, Phoenix." I wiped some sweat from my eye. It was sweat, I swear. I forced myself to breathe deeply. I was so not going to cry right now. Making air move in and out of my lungs, I took in my surroundings.

I was in a jungle, again, but this jungle was not as open or dry as the place Benyst called home. This jungle was thick with vines, and the air was so moist each breath felt like soup moving in and out of my lungs. I unzipped my jacket and dug a hair elastic out of a pocket. Humidity and my hair do not get along. I twisted my hair into a high bun and wrapped it in the elastic. Between my hair being up and my jacket open, the hilt of the sword was visible above my collar. It couldn't be helped, it was way too hot to do otherwise.

"Well, now for the legwork."

I sighed a heavy soupy sigh, wondered briefly if this was how Sid felt when he breathed, and then headed off in a random direction. I had no idea where I was and no idea where Silverwood would be, but I knew Travellers. If someone entered their territory, they'd investigate. Especially if that territory belonged to a member of the Guard and extra-especially if the intruder was me.

Technically, Silverwood and I had never met. He knew

my past self very well, though; he had been there when I was Bound to the Ground and again when I was Banished. In the vision my wings showed me, he had looked devastated by the Banishment. Silverwood couldn't help me then, but maybe he could help me now.

Stumbling on a particularly moss-covered log, I grabbed at a nearby branch to stabilize myself and came away with a sap covered hand. "Gross," I mumbled, scanning the trees for a leaf broad enough to wipe my hand on. I spotted one a few feet ahead and walked towards it. Three steps later, I stumbled again. This time I went down hard, ripping the knee of my jumpsuit. "Shit!" I got to my feet and checked the rip, red flesh showed beneath it. "Ah, double shit," I muttered angrily. "What did I trip on?" I asked no one in particular as I scanned the ground. I had tripped on a clear and flat piece of jungle path. "Just excellent." I wiped sweat from my brow and unwittingly deposited a sizeable amount of sap on my face. Grunting with rage, I ripped a leaf from a nearby plant, checked it for bugs and then wiped my face and hand. Suddenly my feet were knocked out from under me, and I was on my ass.

Okay, things were now weird and bad.

The landing had been hard enough to knock the wind out of me, and I scrambled on the muddy ground as I tried to find my attacker and refill my lungs. The air was so warm that it moved easily through my constricted throat, loosening the tight muscles as it went. When I could use my voice again, I called out.

"Okay, coward! Show yourself! Do it quickly, and I won't kick your ass quite as hard."

Subtle, that's what they call me; subtle.

A sound filled the clearing. It was like tiny leaves rustling in a high wind. A strange sound, and if I didn't know any better, I'd swear it was laughing. I stood in the centre of the clearing and tried to track the sound. It was moving around me in a fast circle. The laughter, for I was sure now that's what it was, sounded to my left. I spun towards it, and it moved, now somewhere to my extreme right.

"Afraid to face me?" I asked the laughter, which grew louder. "Yeah, this is hilarious!"

I pulled quickly at the energy in my core, and a tiny ball of it appeared in my hand. It was bright blue and pulsed slightly. The laughter sounded again to my left, and I threw the ball in its direction. It struck the ground, and a quick burst of blue flame erupted. I could feel the heat from the blaze, but the surrounding plants were unscathed. The balls were just for this asshole. Hmm, that didn't sound right. Anyway... I pulled another energy ball into my hand and waited for the laughter. It was moving in an arc behind me and, trying to guess its destination, I tossed the ball in front of it.

The plan worked.

Sort of.

The laughter became a sharp squeal, and the smell of burning wood filled the clearing. As I took that in something hit me behind the knees, and I toppled forward. My wings didn't have enough time to flap, and I went down hard. My hands couldn't get a grip on the slick ground and went out in front of me, landing me face down in the mud. Some of it went in my mouth.

Son of a bitch must pay.

The laughter, now louder than ever, was right beside me. With anger in my heart and mud in my mouth, a ball of energy, bigger than the others, appeared instantly in my hand. I chucked it as hard as I could in the laughter's direction. I heard the creature gasp as it realised it had no time to escape. I watched the ball travel into the brush, its blue glow flashing through the leaves. The creature's gasp became a scream. This would be over in a moment.

"Enough!" A deep voice like the creaking hull of a grand ship suddenly filled the clearing.

The ball of energy froze in midair and then exploded in a shower of sparks and flame. Shielding my eyes, I rolled away from the blast. When it had cleared, I looked up. There, his bark shining with dew and a crown of branches reaching high into the canopy was Silverwood.

22

"Zip, get out here!" he barked. Literally, it sounded like bark. There was a rustling in the bushes, and then a most unusual creature stepped into the clearing.

It looked like a sapling, but it had legs and arms and a tiny face. A tiny face with a wicked smile spread across it. It stood about two feet high, and as it got closer, I could see that instead of fingers and toes, it had soft pink roots. It was a mini Silverwood.

"Sorry, Grandpa," the little guy laughed, and that annoying rustling sound filled my ears again.

"Zip, do not be so rude," Silverwood gestured at me. "Apologize."

"Saaawwwwweeee," Zip said in my direction, distorting the word as only a petulant child can.

I was still sprawled out on the muddy ground. It was not fun, and the apology sucked, so I just stared at the kid. Um, sapling.

"That's the best you will get, I'm afraid," Silverwood said.

"Okay," I replied dryly.

"Grandpa?" The little guy was looking scared. Good.

"Go straight home, Zip. I will speak to you later."

"But Grandpa...." the kid whined.

"Now!"

The command held power and Zip wisely ran off. Both Silverwood and I watched him go.

"The strong ones are always the hardest to handle." Silverwood looked at me. "As you know."

"Right. Well, I guess I'll get up now."

I tried to move gracefully to my feet and then realised there was no point. Since I was already covered in mud and scratches, getting up in a ladylike fashion seemed pointless. So I clamoured to my feet and faced Silverwood. We were practically the same height.

"I thought you'd be taller," I said.

"I'm sorry to disappoint you."

Oh, this was getting off to a lovely start.

"I'm sorry, Silverwood. I'm not usually this rude when I meet people."

Silverwood laughed. Zip may have sounded like a rustle of leaves, but Silverwood laughed like thick oak planks being slapped together.

"I doubt that," he smiled warmly. "I am sorry about my grandson. He should not have teased you like that," the smile became a smirk, "even if you are an uninvited guest."

"Yeah, I'm sorry about that too. Honestly, I didn't know I was coming here until a little while ago."

"Why are you here, Phoenix?" His face was so open and calm. The branches stretching from his head swayed, making a soothing sound.

"I need you to tell me how to get to The Archer's home."

"Oh!" His trunk creaked as he rocked back, taking in the question. "Oh, Phoenix, I cannot answer that question."

"Is this more forbidden Guard crap?" I shot back.

This entire trip had become a nightmare. First the stuff with Benyst, then that crazy tree kid, and now Silverwood.

"No, no, Phoenix. You misunderstand me." He raised his branch like arms in a gesture of supplication. "I do not know where his home is."

"Do you know anyone who does?" I pleaded. He sighed heavily, sadly.

"I am afraid I do not."

"Oh."

My lower lip trembled. I mustered my will and forced it to stop. I would not cry. No way. I was a big, tough Traveller and I could handle this.

"Phoenix, what is wrong?"

Normally I would ignore such a question from someone I barely knew, but he said it so kindly, with such compassion, that I felt compelled to pour my heart out to him.

And I did just that. I told him about the Bounty, Yeren, that I couldn't find Archer, the Minion attacks, what happened in the City in the Trees and how I'd found the portal at the train station. Hell, I even told him about my brother's birthday party. The only things I'd left out were the Gargoyles and my sword. Even in my emotional state I felt they needed to be kept secret. When I'd cried myself out, he placed his rooty hand on my shoulder. The gentle pulse of the roots soothed me as he spoke.

"That is a lot for even the strongest Traveller to handle."

"Yeah," I whispered, half to myself.

"I may not know where The Archer is, but I know two things that may help you." He held up one pink, rooty finger. "One, you are powerful, and with or without The Archer, you will overcome these trials." A second flange joined the first. "And two, I can teach you how to find him."

Hope filled my spirit. Green sparks flashed behind my eyes.

"You can?"

"Yes." He started walking deeper into the jungle. "Follow me."

Things were looking up.

23

I followed the moving tree through the jungle. We walked up steep hills, slid down more than one hillside, and crossed a stream. I was tempted to make a Ghostbuster joke but found myself preoccupied with the way Silverwood's 'toes' wriggled and plumped up in the water. Besides, he probably doesn't even know what a movie is, let alone how good bustin' can make one feel.

When the mud on my pants had dried, and I felt as if I could walk no further, Silverwood finally stopped.

"Here we are."

'Here' looked like every other inch of the jungle I'd seen and I told him so.

"Look without your eyes," he replied.

"Excuse me?"

"As you did at the train station, Phoenix. Open your heart and see the world around you."

"My heart?"

"Your heart, your power. They are the same."

This was getting very zen. Silverwood moved to a fallen log and settled himself into a seated position. Sitting in full lotus was not an option for the tree, so he stretched his trunk-legs out in front of him and closed his eyes.

"Sit, Phoenix. Breathe."

I rolled my eyes.

"I saw that."

"Seriously?"

He lifted one eyelid, a smirk on his face.

"Just kidding."

I shook my head at him. He smiled more broadly and then returned to his meditative pose. I looked around the clearing, searching for a place to sit. I may have been filthy, but I didn't want to be uncomfortable. The only place to sit seemed to be beside Silverwood. He was quite an imposing figure sitting there on the log. His arms were out in front of him, hands resting on his bark covered legs. He sat up straight, actually I'm not sure if he even had a waist to bend, and as I looked at him, the branches emanating from his skull seemed to stretch and breathe in the moist air. I perched on the log beside him.

Up close I could hear him breathing, air moved smoothly and deeply in and out of his body. Just underneath the sound of his breaths, the slight creaking of his wooden body was audible. I closed my eyes and tried to match his breaths. I focused on the inhalation and drew the oxygen as deeply into my lungs as my ribs would allow. When I felt I could hold no more, I let the breath leave me slowly, drawing out the process of exhalation, making sure my body did not collapse as my lungs deflated. A slight pause and then I brought fresh air into my body, repeating the process.

We sat there breathing together for some time. It was peaceful and yet as time wore on my mind grew more alert. A slight tingle sounded in my centre and rather than force it into being, I merely observed it and continued breathing. The energy grew on its own, and within five breaths it was a swirling joyful mass that moved through my torso.

"Let it touch your eyes," Silverwood whispered.

My energy heard the instruction and instantly the space behind my eyes, in the centre of my skull, tingled. Sparkling purple energy swirled and I could feel the connective tissue that held my eyes in place become invigorated by this fresh source of power. The energy twisted and coated the spheres that were my eyes, purple light spun beneath my lids. The power leaked out through my lashes to coat the skin around my eyes. The muscles there loosened, and I felt the fine lines around my eyes disappear. The energy continued to coat my skull, seeking the fine muscular pathways that allowed expression and the focus of vision. It Travelled over my scalp and down my neck before swooping around to flow into my mouth and down my throat, back to its source.

I didn't know if this movement of energy would be visible to a passerby or if this magical purple essence was a trick of my mind. It did not matter. The power felt wonderful. I neither pushed nor controlled it, I simply let it be. I breathed and breathed, and with every inhalation, I felt stronger and clearer of heart and mind.

"You are ready," Silverwood's soft voice touched my ears, "Open your eyes."

Everything around me shimmered with its own internal light. What was hidden from my normal eyes revealed itself to my power infused vision. I could discern the aura of every plant around me. I saw how they intermingled. I saw the light of the various insects and animals as they moved around us.

"It's beautiful," I whispered.

"Look up."

With a gentle effort, I lifted my eyes and was so shocked by what I saw that I jumped to my feet.

The clearing was ringed in portal openings. There were at least ten encircling us, each composed of tiny pieces of light that swirled and undulated like a school of fish.

"Holy crap."

Silverwood's body groaned as moved to stand beside me.

"It is impressive, isn't it?"

I looked over at the wise old tree; his smile was radiant as he looked around the clearing.

"So many possibilities, Phoenix. So many choices."

"Yes, but how does this help me find Archer?"

His twiggy eyebrow arched at my use of Archer's informal name.

"Hmm," he said, "why do I feel there is more between you two than you are telling me." I opened my mouth, about to come up with some kind of mild lie about what Archer and I are to each other, but he cut me off with a chuckle. "Tis no matter, Phoenix. I think you will find us trees far more open-minded than the others in the Void."

He gently patted my shoulder. For the first time I saw him register the sword at my back. His eyes lingered on it for a moment, and then he shook his head.

"You have changed so much."

That line was getting old, yet no less heartbreaking. I looked away. How could the things that had happened to me do anything but change me? Were the personalities of Travellers typically so static that nothing phased them? These were all questions for another day; right now I had to get on with my plan.

"How do I find him?" I asked, my tone stern. This seemed to snap Silverwood back to the task at hand.

He took my arm and walked me to the centre of the

clearing before retreating to the far edge. "Close your eyes. Good, now clear your mind. Return to your breath and allow it to wipe your mind clear of desire and thought."

I centred my weight over my feet and softened my knees. I drew in a breath and forced it down deep into my body. When I was full to the brim with warm jungle oxygen, I released it slowly. As I exhaled, I calmed my thoughts and focused on the air itself. It was easier this time. My body knew what I wanted, and within a few breaths, my mind was filled with nothing but the energy swirling through me.

Silverwood's deep voice filled the clearing.

"Now, picture The Archer. Picture him more clearly than you have ever pictured anything before."

I did as Silverwood instructed. I imagined Archer so clearly that I could smell the scent of his skin, see the lustre of his pearlescent silver flesh, see every chiselled muscle of his chest, the smooth ridges of his six-pack stomach.

I could feel my face getting warm, very warm.

"Reach into your heart and lay your feelings for him over the image."

This was much harder. What had been only blissful puppy love a few days ago was now far more complicated. He must have heard about the Bounty by now, and yet he was still missing. The sword, a powerful gift, was growing warm at my back as I thought of him. There were so many opposites at play, I felt my heart would burst with feeling.

"Archer." The word escaped my mouth in a whimper that held sorrow and lust.

"Good," Silverwood whispered. "Now reach out to the surrounding portals, feel their energies against your hands. Look for his essence in their power."

With my eyes still closed, I raised my arms out in front of me and walked slowly around the clearing. Although I could not see, my heart was in control, and it led me in a thorough exploration of the ten portals. I approached each and moved my hands over the surface of undulating energy, careful not to touch it. The tiny points of light were visible through my eyelids, and I watched them swirl before me. The first eight portals held nothing for me. Yes, I could have moved easily through them and into another world, but they did not call to me. I was losing faith in the process when I came to the ninth portal.

I reached a hand towards it and instantly a shock of energy whipped through my body. I cried out softly as I rocked back and forth in the aftermath.

"Search it, Phoenix. There is nothing to fear."

Trusting in Silverwood, I raised my hands to the portal. The lights seemed brighter. As the ball of light rolled before my hands, a snapshot of the Archer standing in a stone room filled my mind.

"He's here!" I whispered. "I can see him."

"Then what are you waiting for?" Silverwood gently replied.

The energy portal drew closer to me.

"Nothing." I turned towards Silverwood. Even with my eyes closed I could see the light of his power. "Thank you."

"You are most welcome."

I turned back to the portal, and it slid down around me, sucking me into itself, and with my eyes closed, I Travelled.

24

———

I could sense the cold stone surrounding me even before I opened my eyes.

I stood in a small alcove, every inch made of grey stone. The floor, the ceiling, the walls, everywhere I looked my eyes met by icy grey stone. It was oppressive.

I poked my head out of the alcove and surveyed my surroundings. I was in the middle of a long hallway. Long being an understatement. From where I stood it seemed to stretch into infinity with no apparent lefts or rights. Big flaming torches were spaced along the walls, their flames so massive they licked the ceiling high above them.

This place had two things going for it; creepy and weird. An excellent combo to take the girlfriend home to.

"Just great," I mumbled to myself, "Maybe it gets better."

Unconvinced, and making an entirely random choice, I turned left and started walking. I passed other alcoves as I walked; some were empty while others held old, discarded pieces of clothing. I realised that I would get very lost if I didn't mark the alcove I'd come from. So I grabbed a piece of clothing at random and hurried back to where I'd started. I was worried I wouldn't recognise it in this maze of niches, but it was clear which I had come from. My footprints stood out against the thick dust that covered the ground.

"Dust?"

That didn't seem right. If this was Archer's home why was there dust all over the entryway? The foot traffic would stop it from forming. Wouldn't it? I checked the alcoves on either side; they were also coated with dust. To verify my footprints, I stepped a foot onto the dust-covered floor. Yep, it matched. I had come out of this alcove. Hoping it would be easy to spot, I spread out the piece of clothing I'd grabbed on the floor of the alcove. As I lay out the cloth, I discovered that I'd taken an old, yellowing shirt with a giant blood stain right in the middle.

"Oh, this just gets better and better."

I was trying to stay light, but my hands were shaking. I quickly draped the shirt across the floor of the niche. It lay there, its big blood stain staring up at me.

"Well, that'll be easy to spot." I tried to force a chuckle, but my throat wouldn't work. I tore my gaze from the shirt and continued walking down the hall.

As I asked myself 'what the hell is this place?' for the hundredth time, an even wider hallway opened up on my right. I jumped back from the entrance and tried to calm my now hammering heart. "This is why I'm here," I reminded myself. Then, with a deep breath that did very little to chill me out, I stepped into the hallway.

There were a couple of things that differentiated it from the previous hall; the first was the size, it was at least twice as wide; the second was the sound of screaming that came from somewhere deep within the stone maze.

"Oh shit," I whispered.

I took a few hesitant steps forward. A man screamed long and hard, another shouted words I could not discern.

"Oh, double shit."

I had to get out of here. This was a really, really bad idea. And if Archer was here, well, I didn't want to know. This was a side of him I knew nothing of, and I wanted it to stay that way. I started backing away from the screams, wondering, in a panicked way, if Archer and I really had a future together.

"What are you doing here?"

I think the only reason I didn't scream was that I had gone to that little-known place beyond fear. That place where your body has been so confused by the choices of fight or flight that, stuck in an infinite loop, it shuts down. The screaming in front of me and the strange voice behind me were too much, I froze.

"I said, what are you doing here?"

The voice went to grab my arm, but the moment their skin touched mine, my brain and body reunited and I spun around, adrenaline filling my veins.

"None of your business," I spat. Not very tough, but hey, I was speaking.

I found myself face to face with a female Archer. Her skin was the same shade of silver, her hair a lustrous black and her body just as muscular. Her hair was long, and she wore a headpiece of silver. She was wearing similar leather pants to his, and a matching bra that stressed just how broad her shoulders were.

"Who are you?" I asked, taken aback by her appearance.

"Has Archer never told you about me, Phoenix?"

She knew my name. That's never a good sign. A glimmer of anger, no, hatred, flickered across her face. She quickly hid it, but not before I had registered it. I had a feeling that if given a chance, this woman would love nothing more than to tear me apart with her bare hands. Like with a dog, never show fear. I answered her question.

"I'm afraid not."

"I am Mhyr." She said the name like it should mean something to me. It didn't.

"Okay."

"You truly do not know me." There was no hint of a question in her tone. "But I know you, Phoenix." There was my name again. "Everyone knows you." She looked me up and down, taking in my jungle covered appearance. "Hmm, I thought you'd be shorter, and less filthy."

This girl was weird. I was already scared, and Mhyr was not helping things. A man's scream, louder than the previous ones, echoed down the hall. I jumped and spun towards the sound.

"My, you are a jumpy bird," Mhyr mocked. The screams appeared not to faze her.

I had to get out of here.

"Yep, that's me, jumpy bird. Ka kaa, ka...." The bird call died in my throat. "Yeah..." Mhyr was looking at me like she was trying to decide if I was a total loser, or food. "I'm going to get going now." I backed up a few steps. "It was, um, nice to meet you."

I waited until I was sure I was out of easy grabbing territory before I turned from her. I had only taken two quick steps when I felt her cold, strong fingers loop around my right forearm.

Moving on instinct, I grabbed her hand with my left and twisted her wrist away from me while simultaneously moving my right arm under and around so I caught her in a wristlock. It took about two seconds, and even in my panicked state, I thought it looked cool. Mhyr gasped, and I pushed into her arm. A slight crack sounded, and she let out a sharp cry. It echoed like a crow's call through the hallway. I dropped her arm and ran.

I could hear her heavy steps bearing down on me. For such a muscular lady, she sure was fast. Trying to lose her, I ran down a random hallway that appeared at my left. This one was also lined with alcoves, and I ducked into one and flattened myself against the stone. I heard Mhyr enter the hall. She took slow, even steps.

"I can feel your presence, Phoenix." She whispered the words, which was weird. "And if I can, the others will soon. You are in danger here." As she said the word danger, new screams bounced down the hall. I whimpered. If I made it out of here alive, I was going to kill Archer.

I could hear Mhyr approaching my ill-conceived hidey-hole. There was nowhere to go. I was beyond screwed. She stepped casually in front of me. Her right wrist was swollen, point for Phoenix.

"We need to get you out of here."

"Huh?" I was so shocked by her words that I could not form a coherent response.

"Yes, I'm trying to help you, bird-girl. You are making it very difficult for me." She held up a swollen wrist. "I will give you a pass on this, mainly because I'm impressed you got me so easily, and get you out of here. Archer would have my head if I let anything happen to you in our tunnels. But..." She braced herself against the walls of the alcove, I could hear her damaged wrist grind as she leant into me, forcing me back as I tried to shrink into the stone. Another round of screams echoed through the halls. She smiled at the sound. "Know this, bird-girl, in another time, another place, I would tear out your heart and let you watch it beat while you died." More screams, they covered my whimpers.

"And that is nothing compared to what they would do to you."

Now, I'm a strong person. I've handled some big time situations with grace and aplomb, okay with a dirty mouth and a lot of attitude, but right then with Mhyr's stale breath against my cheek and the sounds of men being tortured, well, I started to cry. It was a soft cry; I didn't sob, and my nose didn't run, tears simply streamed down my face in uncontrolled rivulets. The streams of saline dripped off my chin and down my chest, pooling between my breasts. Myhr took a step back from me, panic on her face for the first time.

"What are you doing?"

"I'm crying." You idiot, I added silently. "Don't tell me you've never seen anyone cry before." I pawed at my eyes, trying to wipe the tears away.

"Of course I have!" Her voice was an angry whisper. "But why are you shimmering?"

"What are you talking about?"

"Look at yourself!"

I looked down at my hands; I wasn't shimmering, but my tears sure were. Everywhere they had touched shimmered like a sprinkling of mother-of-pearl. It instantly made me feel better.

"Cool!"

"No, not cool, not cool at all." Mhyr grabbed my arm and pulled me from the alcove. "Come on, we've got to hurry." I had to trot to keep up with her. "They'll be here soon."

"They?" That word totally brought me back down.

"The others, the ones you heard screaming. They play some brutal games. They will know you are here now and if we do not hurry, they will find you." She looked at me over her shoulder, an evil grin on her face. "You do not want that."

"Shit."

She laughed.

"Exactly."

We were back at the main hallway where she had found me; we turned the corner and Myhr ran, dragging me behind her.

"Hurry," she commanded through gritted teeth.

"I am." I'm not a runner, and even the massive amount of adrenaline coursing through my veins wouldn't turn me into one.

A shout, a man's voice, sounded much closer than any of the screams I had heard. A second and third man responded to him. Footsteps echoed towards us.

"Then you will die!" Myhr grunted.

My wings went ridged at my back; they had no desire to be separated from me again. The reminder of their presence calmed me enough to focus and draw on my power. I called it forth, and green lightning sprang from my heart and filled my bones, coated my muscles, I ran faster. Myhr looked back for me, but I was already at her side. She dropped my hand, and we ran together.

"Hey!" A man's voice sounded behind us.

"Stop!" A second man, then heavy footsteps pounding towards us.

"Left," whispered Mhyr and we turned down the final passageway.

All the alcoves looked the same.

"I don't remember which is Archer's!" I gasped, even with my power behind me my lungs were screaming.

"Seventh on the left." Mhyr was not even winded.

In the back of my mind I wondered why she had committed the location to memory and what, exactly, was her relationship to Archer. In the front of my mind, I was counting alcoves. I was about to pass the sixth when Mhyr shoved me.

"Learn to count, bird!"

She pushed me into the alcove. My feet slipped on the shirt I'd laid out, and I tumbled forward. Mhyr grabbed me by throat and pinned me to the back wall of the niche. I could hear the men at the end of the hall as I struggled to breathe.

"You get one pass with me, bird," spit flew from her mouth with every word, her face contorted with hate. "One pass for him and no more." The men were closer. "They would kill you here and now," she leant in and licked a tear from my cheek. "But I will kill you next time."

She let go with such force that my head smacked against the wall behind me. As I slid into Travel and oblivion, two men, as silvery and muscled as Archer, rushed at Mhyr.

The last thing I saw was her knock them both to the ground.

25

Everything was grey. I looked left and right, stars erupted before my eyes making me grunt with pain, but beneath them all was grey. I was in the Void. A voice sounded above me, a very familiar voice.

"Well, aren't you a ssssight for sore eyesssss..."

I struggled through the blinding pain in my skull and sat up.

"Hello, Mastyx."

"You've got some balls coming here," he laughed. It was a slithering sound. "And I always said you had balls."

"No, you didn't."

"Oh, but I implied it, darling, I implied it."

I was having serious trouble getting up. Mastyx appeared before me and offered me his hand. I took it, and he helped me to my feet. I swayed, and he held me still.

"Would I have dropped you in it with Cosima if I thought you didn't have gigantic balls?" He laughed at his own absurdity.

"So you admit you did that on purpose?" I tried to turn,

and the world spun. I bent forward and braced my arms on my knees, willing myself not to throw up.

"We could debate that all day, darling, but from the looks of you, we have more pressing matters." He touched the back of my head, his fingers came back red. "Yes, I thought I smelled blood." His long snake like tongue zipped from his lipless mouth and licked the blood from his fingers. "You taste wonderful." He reached for my skull again.

"I don't freaking think so." I tried to move away from him, stumbled and fell to my knees. This time I did throw up. Not much, but enough to make my eyes burn, and to realize I had a serious head injury.

"Good lord, darling," Mastyx said, then as an afterthought, he added, "and please note that I am not saying your name, thus preventing a horde of idiots from raining down upon us. Now tell me, darling, what happened to you?"

I wiped snot and vomit from my face with the back of my hand. Mastyx passed me a hanky. The dude walks around naked. Where is he hiding a hanky? I didn't want to know. I was just grateful for the opportunity to wipe my face.

"Mhyr. Mhyr happened to me."

"What!" he sounded shocked. "How in Time did you run into her? She hardly ever leaves the Compound."

"Ah, so that's where I was. The Compound."

Mastyx was on his knees in front of me before the words left my mouth.

"Please don't tell me The Archer took you there."

"If I didn't know better, I'd say you were concerned for my wellbeing."

"You're interesting, I enjoy interesting," he smirked. "I

definitely don't want to see such an interesting creature get her skull bashed in."

"Aw, that's the sweetest thing you've ever said to me," I replied through the acid on my tongue. I crawled away from my pile of vomit and leant against a nearby tree.

I looked out at the scene before me. A sinewy snake man crawled towards me, his body undulating as his forked tongue flicked in and out, scenting the air. But that wasn't the most disturbing thing I saw. That title belonged to the grey: the massive amounts of unending grey that saturated every molecule of the land before me. The sky was an oppressively solid hue, the colour of clouds before a winter storm. The land was a shade darker, and it moved and rippled slowly, I could almost perceive the changes as I scanned the horizon. There were a few trees scattered here and there, all like the one I now leant against; dead and peeling with few leaves and the skeletal appearance of an ageing birch. The Void did nothing to lift my spirits.

Mastyx came to a halt beside me. He stretched out on his side and looked at me with something in his eyes that resembled genuine concern.

"So did Archer take you there?"

"No, that was all me. I didn't do it on purpose though. I was trying to find him, and Silverwood showed me how to read the portals and..."

"Yes, Silverwood, the great trusting tree. Let me guess, he told you to think of your man and then jump into the portal that showed his energy?"

"That's exactly what he said."

"Yes, and that's usually a wonderful plan if you're looking for puppies or rainbows, but when you're trying to track a creature as dangerous as The Archer, you need to be more careful."

Dangerous? Archer was dangerous? I'd never considered that before, but after seeing that stone clad hell they call the Compound, it didn't seem that farfetched.

"Don't look so hurt, darling," Mastyx drawled. "Did you really think you knew everything there was to know about him?"

"Well..."

"Oh please," he laughed again, it sounded like nails on a chalkboard and chewing tinfoil had a baby. "You get so angry when everyone else is surprised that you've 'changed.'" He made air quotes. It really showed off the webbing between his fingers. "But you don't allow others a similar courtesy." He sat up and pierced me with his yellow eyes. "You weren't even in the loop before your Banishment. You really know nothing about anyone." His voice dropped to a sibilant whisper, "Who are the people you trust?"

He meant his words to shock me, but they didn't. The logic was too plain for me to hide behind fear. I didn't know any of these creatures. Look at what had happened with Noiryn and Benyst; a few days ago I would never have predicted that I could piss them both off so badly. And Sid, that had been conundrum from the start. I had known him longer, spent more time with him than any of the others, and still, he betrayed me. At least I'd had Yeren's number from the beginning.

Mastyx was looking at me like he expected me to cry. I let my lower lip quiver and looked at him with the biggest, most innocent eyes I could muster.

"So, you're the only friend I have?" He looked pleased; I put on my baby voice and continued. "Will you take care of me? Pwetty pwease?"

"Ha!" he snorted and sat up. "Amusing, were you a comedienne in your human life?"

"You're not scaring me, Mastyx. You're not telling me anything I haven't told myself."

Using the tree as a support, I got to my feet. My vision stayed steady, and I didn't throw up again, which was good. My head was pounding in a borderline tolerable kind of way, so I continued talking.

"I don't really know any of you, and worst of all, I don't really know myself. I only just got these." I flapped my wings, rising a few inches off the ground, and then settling down again. It made my head spin. "I'm just starting to figure out how to use them. And now I've got this freaking Bounty on my head."

"Ah yesssss, the Bounty."

"Is Cosima behind it?"

"Cosima!" Mastyx laughed so hard he pounded his fists on the dry grey earth. "Cosima..." He licked a tear from his eye. "You really are quite funny."

"So she isn't behind it?"

"She can't keep track of her own life, let alone organize the entire Void in a Bounty hunt. I also don't think she's capable of the power it would take to drain you of yours."

"I thought she wanted me dead after I stole that skin for you and kicked her ass."

"Oh, she'ssssss mad at you," Mastyx hissed, "But her anger will burn itself out. She'll probably attack you if the opportunity presents itself. But as I said; you can take her." He paused and scrutinized me. "Especially now that you have that lovely sword."

Crap. The sword. In the craziness of the last couple hours, I had forgotten to keep it hidden. I looked myself over; my coat was open and flapping in the ever-present breeze, my hair was half out of its ponytail and matted with blood, and the hilt of the sword was visible. I slowly did up my jacket and pulled the elastic from my hair. I attempted to run my fingers through it, but there was too much blood. I probed my scalp with my fingers and winced when I found a large gash on top of a sizeable bump.

"Stop fretting, darling, it's nothing you can't heal," Mastyx sighed.

"Yeah, but I probably need stitches. Where am I going to get those?"

"Stitchessss?" The scaly ridge above his eyes rose with scepticism. "Are you not the great healing Traveller? Why don't you run some power through it or something?"

Whoa. I hadn't thought of that.

"Right, right, just testing you." I drew energy into my hand.

"Not here!" Mastyx shouted as his hand encircled my wrist. "Are you crazy, girl? You use your power here, and you'll be strung up and delivered to your hunter in moments."

His face was very close to mine. As his tongue flicked, I could feel the air move against my lips. I may not know all of him, but I knew the look in his eyes. They were full of genuine concern.

"Who put out the Bounty?" I asked in a hushed voice.

"If I knew, I would tell you," he replied. The moment stretched out between us while he held my wrist. "You are so very interesting." There was a strange tone to his voice, and I couldn't place its origin. I opened my mouth to ask him about it, and he sprang back. "You must get home and heal that grotesque lump on the back of your head." He was back to his usual self, all pomp and poise and wicked grins.

"Okay." The pain in my skull was now a deep throbbing pulse that made my blood feel thick and lazy. "I'll be off then."

"Darling, you really know nothing about what you are." He came to stand beside me and pointed to something in the distance. "Use one of those or the others will track you."

He was pointing at a stream.

"That does not look fun," I replied.

"And it isn't." We walked towards the stream. "But you really don't have a choice right now. If you Travel from here, they'll track you, and if you heal that cut here, they'll track you."

He grabbed my head and sniffed the back of my skull. I pushed him away.

"Gross, Mastyx."

"Maybe, but by the smell of things that wound will fester if you don't get to it soon."

"Can you heal yourself?"

"No." He looked away. "I cannot."

We had reached the stream; the water was jet black, and its surface looked like a fast-running river frozen in time. There were currents visible on the surface, but they did not move. I had one more question for Mastyx before I made him explain how this whole Travelling by stream thing worked.

"So what happens to the creatures here that can't heal themselves, what do they do if they're injured?"

"We come to see you."

I didn't have time to register my shock at his answer because no sooner than the words had left his mouth; he pushed me into the stream. He called after me in a laughing, sing-song voice as the black water sucked me down.

"Just think of home, darling, think really hard!"

26

Holy crap, it was cold. It was colder than anything I had ever felt in my life. It clawed at my skin, the pores themselves trying to rebel from the icy attack. It was thicker than regular water, and my quickly numbing limbs fought against its molasses-like texture. I tried to find the surface, but everywhere I looked was the ebony abyss of the stream. I flapped my wings and kicked with my legs as my lungs burned. The stream was so narrow; the sides had to be close; I thought. This is the Void, another thought answered, nothing is as it seems. I was moving more slowly in the icy darkness. A voice, louder than the others, rolled through my brain; if you don't get your head together, you will die here.

"Just think of home, darling, think really hard!"

Was Mastyx right? Was that all it would take? Just think of my beloved home, and I would be free of this pitch black hell? The cold had made my arms and legs numb, and I could no longer feel my wings. I forced myself to stop fighting the water and to go limp. The water supported me, and I tried to ignore my desperate desire to breathe. That could wait, I told myself.

I remembered what Silverwood had taught me and called forth a clear image of my home. I pictured it as it looked from my gate, every window, every brick, the greenhouse, the big carved doors, and my gargoyles. I went through every detail and let them feed my heart as I floated in the darkness.

A giant popping sound, like a plug being pulled, reverberated through the water and I started to spin.

It was slow at first, a smooth circle that made my arms and wings rise in the water. It was disorientating in the complete darkness, and I started to get nauseous again. The water kept swirling, faster and faster, and soon my body was drawn out into a tight line, my arms beside my head and my wings stretched above me, their tips touching, feathers splayed. As the speed increased, it became apparent that I was also being pulled down, as if through a massive drain. My body wanted to fight the current, and my brain battled between panic and resignation. Faster and faster I swirled, drawn ever deeper into the inky black water. The speed seemed to double, and the pressure of the water on my body pushed out the last bit of oxygen I held in my lungs. I couldn't go on much longer, but there was nowhere to go. No escape. I would die here in this swirling pit of liquid despair.

My lungs screaming in agony, I couldn't fight the impulse to breathe. Thick icy water filled my mouth and consciousness left me.

27

ir hit my lungs like a train; the warmth painful as it forced its way into my frozen lungs. I coughed, and water flowed from my mouth. I struggled to open my eyes, and I saw jet black fluid pooled beneath me. I choked down air as quickly as I could. With the air came fire. It hurt like hell. My fingers felt like they were submerged in flame, my wings blistering as my toes melted. Through the pain, I tried to take in my surroundings. I saw a sandy path covered in dappled sunlight; I heard birds.

I was home.

Well, not quite. I had to get through the gate before I would be safe and in my current condition, there was no way I could walk there. So I did what I had to do. I crawled.

Unfortunately, I am no stranger to crawling. The last time I'd had to crawl like this, I was trying to save Archer. This time I was saving myself. I needed to get warm, fast. With quaking limbs, I put one hand in front of the other. My wings were limp and dragged alongside me, I looked back at them to find that my feathers were ruffled and some were missing. I took one half-numb yet burning hand and reached up. My nearly useless hand found the hilt of my sword, and I moaned with relief. This sound forced the last vestiges of water from my lungs and once again I found myself in a pool of jet black water.

I made myself keep moving, my wings leaving a trail behind me in the sandy path. I could see the gate up ahead, and I redoubled my efforts, making my burning toes dig into the sand to push me forward. I got to the edge of the gate and placed my hand across the line. It screamed with pain, and I pulled it back. The warm waterfall feeling of the gate that usually met my skin now felt like a thousand blades against my defrosting flesh.

I pushed myself up with my arms and sat back on my heels and looked at the gate. The wicker arch that framed the gateway was about a foot deep. If I tried to crawl through it, the pain would be overwhelming. I didn't think I would make it. The only way this would work was if I threw myself through the gate, making the agony timeframe as short as possible.

My legs were still too weak for walking, but maybe they could keep me standing for a few seconds. I grabbed the wicker arch, careful not to pass into the pain zone, and using a hand over hand technique, pulled myself to standing.

I positioned myself to jump through the gate. I let go of the arch, bending my knees to leap, but the weight of my limp wings pulled me backwards, and I pitched forward to counterbalance, over corrected and fell forward towards the gate.

My upper body passed through the curtain of tiny knives and was soon clear of the gate. However, my lower half was still in the gateway. I screamed and tried to kick my legs free, but I couldn't move them. I clawed at the ground, trying to pull myself forward. But I didn't have the strength. I laid there and screamed. And screamed. And screamed.

I don't know how long I screamed for, it could have been an hour, it could have been sixty seconds. I lay there screaming in pain until two pairs of tiny stone hands slipped under my arms and pulled me free.

I think I said thank you before I passed out.

28

The sea was angry with me. It knew my sins and gladly took the body I gave it.

The waves rolled over me, dragging me down and then throwing me up into the air so I spun in the cold spray only to smack down again on its unyielding surface. I ached all over; I could feel cracked bones rub against each other. Any moment now my neck would break, and I would be helpless as the water pulled me under.

How much longer would it make me wait?

29

———————

"**S**witch!"

It was a hushed command full of urgency. It pulled me from my awful dream, and as I regained consciousness, I could hear the quick patter of stone feet on the tile. The undulating light and warmth of a fire licked at my eyelids. I opened my eyes a tiny amount and saw a small stone gargoyle jump into the flames and settle in amongst the burning logs. At the same moment, I felt a warm, firm creature wriggling under the blankets that covered me.

"What's going on?" My mouth was paper and the sound so reedy and small I wasn't sure they would hear me.

"You're awake!" Grog cried from his seat in the fire.

"Yay!" chorused Brog from under the blankets. He crawled to the edge and stuck out his tiny dented skull. "We thought we'd lost you!"

"Back to work, Brog," Grog chided.

The tiny gargoyle yelped, dashed under the blankets and settled against my stomach. I felt like the marrow in my bones had turned to ice, and the warmth of his stony body was wonderful. I patted Brog's head, and he snuggled in closer.

"So what happened? How did you guys get me here?"

Here was in front of my fireplace. The boys had pulled over a stack of pillows, which I now lay on, and it felt like every blanket in the house was piled on top of me. They had built an enormous fire in the massive fireplace and Grog stoked the flames from his seat within them.

"We carried you, lady." Grog replied. "It wasn't easy, it was hard to get your wings to stop flopping around."

"One of them hit me in the face!" Brog called happily from under the blankets.

"Thank you, guys. I don't know what would have happened to me if you hadn't been there."

"Eventually, the gate would have burned through your legs," Grog said grimly.

"Wow. That would have been bad."

"Yes, lady." He looked so strange sitting calmly as flames licked his face. "What were you doing that would cause these injuries?"

"Injuries?"

"Yes, the hypothermia and the cut on your head."

"Right, I'd forgotten about that one."

"My lady, what is going on?" Grog stood, the flames framing his barrel chest.

"You can't ask her that!" cried Brog from deep within the blankets.

"Switch!"

Grog practically shouted the word. Both Brog and I jumped, but he did as he was told and crawled from the blankets and into the fire. Grog shuffled past him as he spoke.

"Yes, I can, Brog," he came over and settled on top of the

blankets, draping as much of himself as he could over me while still making eye contact. "We have been with you for so long, my lady. If anything happened to you, what would we do?" A pebbled rolled from his eye and hit the floor. The sound of it bouncing along the stone echoed through the room. "We already lost you once, we cannot bear it again." More pebbles. "Please, Phoenix, what is going on?"

Perhaps it was the use of my name, or maybe it was Brog sobbing quietly in my fireplace, I don't know; I felt like a mother hen with a big decision before me. I thought sheltering them from the Bounty was the right thing to do, but I had forgotten about what they had been through with me. I had rescued them, taken care of them and then one day I just didn't come home. And that one day had stretched out to thirty years. I couldn't let that happen again. They had to know about the Bounty; they had to know about the danger I was in. They would be completely alone if anything happened to me.

"All right, I'll tell you what's going on." I took a deep breath to centre myself, I needed to get straight to the point. "Someone has placed a Bounty on my head. The entire Void is aware of it, and they are all after me. I am wanted alive, so that's something." I knew the Gargoyles were made of stone, but at that moment they truly looked like statues. Scared statues. "Guys, it's okay. I know who put out the Bounty and once I've healed these injuries, I'm going after them."

As the words left my mouth, I realised they were true. I knew who put the Bounty out on me. Big G, Greldrom, the ultimate douche bag. He definitely had the power, he'd almost bested me in the Circle, and he had the manpower to find me, his Minions had proven that. Yep, it had to be him. Which meant there was only one place I had to go.

"The City of Caves," Grog whispered.

"What?" Man, this gargoyle was quick.

"I can see it in your eyes." As he continued, Brog crawled from the fire and joined his brother. "You think, Greldrom is responsible for the Bounty and you're going to his kingdom to confront him."

Brog let out a tiny yelp and stuffed his stony fingers in his mouth.

"I don't think Greldrom did it, I know he did. He's the only one with the power to make it happen." I sat up. The room didn't spin, and my stomach stayed calm, yay me. "I'm going to the City of Caves because I have no other option. I will not hide here and pray this blows over, I will attack it head on. I will not be a prisoner in my home." I pulled back the blankets, and the gargoyles scattered. I sighed and tried to sound as reassuring as possible. "I will be fine, maybe not good or great, but fine. I've survived worse things."

"I don't know if you have," Grog's voice was quiet. "The City of Caves is a terrible place."

"Yes, Grog," I admonished, "You keep telling me that."

I got to my feet. There were a few lingering stars in my eyes, but on the whole, I just felt stiff and sore. I looked at my wings; they were still heavily ruffled, and more feathers were missing than I remembered. I touched the back of my head and found an egg-sized lump there. That would have to go.

"Guys, when I was here before, did I have a special place or something that I used to heal my own injuries?"

The gargoyles looked at each other. Brog snickered.

"What do you think the greenhouse is for?"

"Oh, right."

I left the two gargoyles giggling on the hearth.

30

I had spent little time in the greenhouse. In the few weeks that Archer and I spent here, we mainly went from the bedroom to the living room to the gate. As I stepped into the humid room, I wondered why we'd ignored it.

It was a phenomenal space. The glass walls were densely covered in vines that reached all the way to the vaulted glass roof sixteen feet above. The vines weaving in and out of each other created a latticework of textures in various shades of green. At the ceiling, cables spanned the width of the room, and the vines continued along them, making the sunlight stream through in slices to the floor below.

I stepped barefoot onto the grassy floor. The ground was soft and yielding, like a field after a spring rain. I dug my toes into the grass; it felt marvellous. A winding path led through the multitude of flowering plants, shrubs and trees that filled the body of the greenhouse. I followed it through twists and turns towards a central clearing that was the heart of the space. Amongst the rustic plants, I passed lovingly tended flower beds and beautifully groomed bushes, and for the first time, I wondered who was taking care of this amazing space. It wasn't me; I had barely been in here since I left my mortal life, yet here was a very well-tended greenhouse. A big question for another time, I thought as my bruised head gave a lurching throb.

I stood the middle of the clearing and took a few deep breaths to centre myself. I turned slowly, taking in my surroundings, deciding the best way to position myself. I noticed enormous chunks of rock on either side of the clearing. They were placed across from each other, and if I lay between them, I would be in a straight line bisecting the clearing. This was no mere coincidence; these rocks were here for a reason. I'd placed them here before my human life, and I would trust myself.

I stretched out on the ground. The clearing was perfectly round and large enough for me to stretch my arms above my head and for my wings to splay out beneath me. The ground was so soft and yielding that even with the wings, lying on my back was comfortable. I made a few playful grass angels and was reminded strongly of that da Vinci picture of the guy in the circle-square thing. I wondered if my old self had seen the picture being made. Maybe when things calmed down, I could go check it out.

I closed my eyes and let my body melt into the soft grass. Rather than focus immediately on my injuries, I let my attention wander through my body, checking in with every inch of my aching frame. I directed my breaths deeper and deeper as my energy flowed through me. It swirled through my legs, up and around my spine, down through my arms, up my neck and through my skull. The shimmery presence flowed into my eyes, and they shot open.

There, floating in the air a few feet above me, was an undulating ball of molten gold energy. It hovered, rolling and changing and yet staying the same. I felt it connect with my heart and a sense of calm and healing flowed from the mass. It was a part of me, a special healing core that I had placed in the magic of this greenhouse so it would always be safe and ready to bring me back to health.

I took a deep breath, and a stream of gold poured down and entered my mouth. As I breathed deeply, it moved through my body and down to my feet. There it coated every tendon, every muscle and sinew with its warm gold nature. As I exhaled, all the tension and pain in my body flowed from my mouth in a red mist that floated out into the trees. I felt the greenery absorb every molecule of pain and convert it into life.

With every breath the gold moved through a new part of me, healing and extracting the red pain. The surrounding trees seemed to grow greener, more full of life as I continued to breathe the crimson mist out into their branches. The golden energy took special time with my heart, wrapping it gently in ribbons of gold that weaved through each other. They flowed like a golden cage, imbuing me with strength and expelling the trauma of the last few days. The screams of that first Minion attack, the stone tunnels with Mhyr, the darkness of the stream; the fear left my body, but the lessons remained. I would not forget what had happened, I simply released the fear.

The wound at the back of my head was the last thing it healed. I felt the fine crack mend and skin re-knit, Mhyr had hurt me more than I realised. When the glob of molten gold had healed every part of me, it moved closer. Hovering inches above my face, its light was so bright that I closed my eyes. It was warm and comforting, and I let my mind wander into sleep as it caressed me.

31

"Phoenix... Phoenix..." A hand touched my face. I swatted at it. "I've missed you." The hand moved down my neck and rested above my heart. A warm tingle shimmered through me.

That got my attention.

I cracked an eyelid. There, with the starry sky and bright green trees behind him, was The Archer. Archer. My Archer.

"Archer," I reached for him.

He came to me eagerly. Our mouths met and sparks flowed between us. I felt every inch of my body respond to him; the simple tingle becoming a rolling wave inside me. He moved until our bodies were laying side by side on the grass. Our mouths still locked, I slowly ran my hands over his naked chest. He caressed the place where my wings joined my body, and I gasped, arching my back in pleasure. He pressed closer to me and the yearning I had felt for him the past few days engulfed my heart. With a great sigh, I rolled on top of him. My wings unfurled to their full glory, every feather now alive and perfect. I reached behind me and undid the straps of my suit; the fabric slipped from my body, and the moist greenhouse air touched my breasts. Groaning, Archer raised himself from the ground and ran his silver lips over me. His hands roved over my body, caressing every curve. I pushed him back to the grass and, with my wings flapping, letting me hover as the golden energy had done, I swiftly pulled his pants from his body.

He is completely silver. Completely.

As I marvelled at his body, he pulled at my clothing and with a grunt and a tug we were naked in the grass together. The sight of my body seemed to soften his heart, and he pulled me tenderly to him. As our flesh met he moaned, his head falling back, his eyes closed. Waves of pleasure flowed through my body. As our passion grew a translucent orb formed around us and cycled through the colours of the rainbow. We moved in perfect rhythm with it. Our breath came faster. The colours flashed brighter. We moved together like we had known each other's body for millennia. Maybe we had. The pleasure grew until I could no longer hold it inside me. I cried out, and power flowed from me, every pore releasing a spark of energy. I watched the tiny particles of light rain down on Archer, and his body bucked with pleasure as my power touched him.

When it was over, we fell back to the grassy floor, panting, sweaty, spent and alive. The surrounding orb dissolved, and we lay there looking at each other as the shimmery energy defused into the trees.

32

"Wow," Archer smiled.

"Really?" I giggled. "Wow?"

"Isn't that what they say in your time?"

"I've really missed you," I said, a touch of seriousness in my voice.

"I know, my love, I have missed you too." A shadow passed behind his eyes.

"What is it?" I sat up and looked down at him. "What's wrong?"

"I don't know how to tell you this." He reached for his pants. Always a bad sign.

"Just tell me."

He was now on his feet and halfway back into his pants. His back was to me, and his perfect ass momentarily distracted me. He zipped up and turned to face me.

"There is a Bounty on your head."

I'm not sure what I was expecting him to say, but it wasn't that. The relief was strange, and I laughed.

"Oh, that!" I stood up and picked up my jumpsuit from

the ground. I was taking a shower before I got dressed again. "I've known about that for a while."

I started down the path back into the main house. The sky was black, time had passed, I needed to get moving.

"You have?" Disbelief was clear in his voice.

"Yes. Yeren told me."

"Yeren?!"

"Yep, while she was attacking me."

"What?!"

"I tried very hard to find you, but I got sidetracked by some minions, and then there was the thing with Myhr."

"Mhyr!?"

I was at the foot of the grand staircase now. Archer grabbed my arm and spun me towards him. It pressed our naked chests together, and my breath quickened.

"Why did you see Mhyr?" he asked in a quiet voice. I could see rage in his eyes.

"I was trying to find you. Silverwood suggested…" He cut me off.

"Silverwood! What.."

"Look!" I shouted as I broke from him. "Are you going to let me tell you what happened or are you going to keep yelling?"

He swallowed audibly and then said through gritted teeth.

"Please continue."

"Let's walk and talk. I need a shower."

He followed me up the stairs. I could feel his eyes on me as I climbed. I'm not going to lie, it was hot. I tried to focus and keep talking. "Silverwood suggested I let the portals guide me to you. And before you ask, Benyst took me to see him." I didn't tell him about the incident with Benyst. Better to leave that out for now, or forever, whatever. "So I jumped into a portal that felt like you, and it took me to a labyrinth of stone hallways. I was trying to find you when I crossed paths with Mhyr."

"What did Myhr say?" His voice was cold and hard as he said her name; I didn't want to see his expression, so I just kept moving. I tossed my ruined jumpsuit on the floor as I made my way into the bathroom.

"She was surprised you'd never mentioned her." I started the shower. "Why have you never mentioned her?"

"She is not worth mentioning." I raised a sceptical eyebrow at him. "She was a part of my life at least a millennium ago, maybe longer. Did she hurt you?"

"Well," I got in the shower, shouting now above the rain of water, "She said you would never forgive her if she didn't help me, so she got me out of there before the others showed up."

"What others?" Archer sounded frightened. I wiped steam from the glass enclosure and looked at him. He looked scared too.

"I didn't get more than a glimpse of them. By the time they got near me, I was ready to Travel."

"Good." His voice was lighter, and it hurt me to have to relay the rest of the tale.

"Not good, actually," I sighed, but it was swallowed up by the sound of the shower. "Basically, she said if she ever saw me again she would kill me. Then she smashed my head into a wall and sent me Travelling."

Archer's hands were suddenly in my wet hair. He eased my skull back and forth in his hands, running his fingers over every inch. I felt a gentle tingle as his energy probed me.

"There is no wound now," he mused. He was now

soaking wet, his pants clung to his muscled thighs, and I became very aware I was still naked.

"Your pants are getting ruined," I whispered.

"They'll be fine," he purred, his face inches from mine. "You healed yourself?"

"Yeah." It was all I could manage.

"Good." He kissed me delicately on the mouth and then stepped from the shower. "What happened after you left the tunnels?"

"Well," I said as I hastily tried to shake off the energy of his kiss. He could be so distracting sometimes. "Let me fill in some gaps first."

I told him about the Minions coming to my parents' house and how they'd tricked me into following them to the City of Trees. I filled him in on my talk with Mastyx and the debacle that was my journey home. When I had finished my tale, I was clean, dressed and ready to go kick some Minion ass.

"You did all that alone. I should have been here for you." He came up behind me as I stood before the bathroom mirror, nestled himself between my wings and wrapped his arms around my waist. "I promise I will never let you face such things alone again."

"Don't promise that crap, Archer." He stepped back. "You can't be here all the time, it's just not possible." I turned to face him. "And honestly, I don't want you to be. I need to do things on my own; I need to know that I can take care of my life and my challenges." I stepped forward and put my hands on his chest. He didn't back away. "When things get too much, it's good to know you're here for me, supporting me and fighting the odd battle with me." He smiled, and I gave him a quick kiss. "But now is one of those times when I need to do something by myself."

He frowned.

"And what is that?"

He was not going to like this.

"I am going to the City of Caves, and I am ending this Bounty once and for all."

I had never seen Archer angry. When we met, he'd been playing the fallen hero card, and since then things in my life had been low key, well until this Bounty thing, so I had only seen him relaxed. I was getting an education in the many facets of Archer's personality now.

He was pissed.

Beyond pissed, actually.

He screamed with rage, which sent me running backwards out of the bathroom and through to the bedroom. He followed me there, the entire time describing in disgusting the detail the terrible things that went on in the City of Caves. He then launched into a rant about how much I meant to him and how dare I risk my life so wantonly when he cared about me so much. I let him keep going until he had blown his anger out and collapsed on the bed, his chest heaving, a thin sheen of sweat on his body.

I spoke in a whisper.

"You're right." He sat bolt upright and stared at me, his silver eyes penetrating me to my core. "You had me convinced ten seconds into your argument. I'm sorry."

He opened his arms to me, and I went to him. We held each other tightly. I didn't want to break the moment, but it had to be done.

"Please come with me," I asked.

"Damn it, Phoenix!" He leapt off the bed. "You still want to go there after all that I've told you!"

It was my turn to get angry.

"He has placed a Bounty on my head!" I tapped my skull.

"This thing, right here! He has sent every creature in the Void after me! I will never be safe until this thing is over once and for all!" My anger moved like a tiny dragon inside me, wanting to break free. "I am going to his lair, and I am dragging him out by the scruff of his neck and ending this. Are you coming with me or not?"

He appraised me, cool, calm, like a general regards a soldier. Can she do this? Can she go into the depths of hell and come out whole?

"I'm coming with you."

"Thank you."

"But first I have to show you something."

"What's that?" This better not be more stall tactics.

"My home."

33

Archer led the way downstairs. But not before he had made me change my boots for something more rugged and put on a leather contraption that he apparently had given me for an occasion such as this.

It was a cross between body armour and a straitjacket. It had sleeves of soft leather with lightweight metal panels on the forearms and biceps. I had to slide my arms into these, and then Archer wrapped the wide pieces of leather attached to the sleeves, around my body. It felt strange going on, but when he was finished, I looked in the mirror and could see what an outstanding piece of clothing it was. The straps fitted perfectly around my wings, protecting their joinings. The pieces continued around my torso, wrapping me with a thick coat of leather that, although supple, would slow down any blade. I noticed, however, as I slipped on the sheath for my sword, that the straps crossed around my breast in a real cleavage enhancing fashion. I gestured at them.

"Nice touch." I slid my blade into its sheath.

"Agreed," he said.

We headed out into the garden, brilliant stars shone above us. I gave the gargoyles, who were frozen at their posts once more, a gentle pat on the head as I passed them. Archer saw me do it and scowled. Since we had decided to go into the Caves, he had been slowly getting his game face on.

"You are so strange, Phoenix."

"Tip of the iceberg, babe."

He sighed audibly and passed through the gate. I could have let myself fear walking through, the thing had nearly killed me a few hours ago, but I didn't let the thought take root. I walked straight through the gate and was rewarded with the pleasant sensation it had always given me.

"Excellent," I whispered to myself.

"Hurry up!" Archer barked. Apparently, he dealt with stress by getting angry. Oh boy, this was going to be fun.

"Archer," I said as I caught up, "You need to simmer down."

"Excuse me?" His voice was low and dark again.

"Chill. We are a team in this, equals, and I will not tolerate you yelling at me just because you are stressing out."

"I am not stressing out!"

"Really? We're getting ready to go into the City of Caves, and you're not stressed? Well, I am. I am super stressed; in fact, I'd go as far to say I'm frightened. Yep, I'm scared shitless, but I'm not yelling at you or getting surly with you. So do me a favour, save it for the fight."

Silence.

I tried to keep the frustration from my voice, but he was making it very difficult.

"Okay?" I prodded.

"Okay." He mumbled.

"Thank you." I strode past him and stood by the portal. Since Silverwood had opened my mind to them, I could see them very clearly now.

"So where are we going?"

"To my home."

These Travellers never change. I said nothing and took Archer's hand. His face was grim as we leapt into the portal.

34

The ground was at an angle. Loose pebbles moved beneath my feet, and I struggled for a few moments as I tried to find my footing. When I felt like I was no longer about to go sliding, I looked up.

We were on the side of a steep hill covered in loose slate shards. Archer was about fifteen feet above me. Here and there I could see miniature stone landslides rolling down the mountain. Yes, mountain was a far more accurate word. As I looked past Archer, I could see that this rise of jagged stone went high into the sky. I couldn't make out the summit, it was covered in clouds, but I could make out where the small stones became enormous boulders. It was very far from where we stood. I was really hoping I didn't have to climb all that way.

"Do you see where the stones become boulders?" Archer called.

Oh crap.

"Yes."

"That is where we must get to."

Double crap.

"Right, um..." I hesitated, it really was insanely far, and I could barely stand on the stone let alone climb it.

"Yes?"

There was concern on Archer's face and, if I wasn't mistaken, a bit of fear. Maybe he was scared to show me his home? Maybe I was the first person he'd brought here? I forced my mind back to reality and tried to respond to him.

"Honestly, Archer, I'm sorry, I don't think I can climb up there."

He gave a quick laugh that echoed off our rocky surroundings then turned and ran, bloody ran, up the rocky hill. He called back to me as he moved with the sure-footedness of a mountain goat.

"That's funny! I thought you could fly!"

Damn it. How do you forget something like being able to fly? I grunted a few minor insults at myself and then took to the air. I flew as hard and as fast as I could up the side of the mountain. I had had little opportunity to fly for long stretches, and the breeze felt fantastic on my face as the powerful muscles in my wings worked their magic. It also gave me time to absorb my surroundings.

Archer's home was definitely on the side of a mountain. But what I had first thought to be a gigantic mountain became dwarfed as I observed the range of mountains around it. They stretched out in a circle, creating an enclosed valley at the base. I could make out a grassy open field and a cluster of trees. I thought I could see tiny human shapes moving around, but I was too far away to be sure.

I beat Archer to the first boulders, but not by much. I sat down on a big rock to catch my breath and watched Archer approach. He was running up the mountain, but this wasn't straight up running. He would use his arms to push himself up and over larger rocks and as he approached me he hopped up onto a boulder and then leapt from rock to rock with the grace of a dancer. The muscles in his chest were visibly firing, and his thighs looked like they would rip through his pants. Was everything this guy did sexy? Yes. Was I complaining? You bet your ass I wasn't.

"Nicely done," I said as he stood before me. He wasn't even breathing hard. The man was a machine. I fought down the tingling that had begun in my core and the blush that had crept up my cheeks.

"Thank you." He was smiling. It had heat to it, and the tingling in me grew.

He reached forward and grabbed my hands. Within a heartbeat, he had pulled me to him and locked his mouth on mine. I kissed him back, and for a few beautiful moments, we stood there steeped in lustful oblivion.

"Wow," I shook my head, trying to clear it. "So where is this home I've been so curious about?"

I felt the energy in him shift so quickly that it made my head hurt. Literally. A sharp pain shot through my skull, I hissed and threw a hand up to my temple. If Archer noticed this, he did not acknowledge it, he just started walking.

"This way."

I followed him through the maze of rock. We twisted through dirt pathways covered in sand so soft my footprints barely registered. We wove through gardens of boulders that had been touched by so many hands that grooves had formed in the rock. And we climbed. Not higher into the mountain, but over rocks too big to be avoided. This was a simple matter for Archer, but not for me. The passages were narrow, and it was difficult for me to manoeuvre with my wings. More than once I had to call Archer back to help me up and over stone. After what seemed like an eternity of scrambling over rock and getting sand in my eyes, I rounded a corner to find Archer standing in front of a large circular stone propped up against a wall of rocky mountainside. He looked so sad, so unsure. I took his hand in mine.

"Am I the first person you've brought here?" I asked softly.

"No."

"Oh, okay." I wasn't expecting that.

"Mhyr has been here."

"Oh, okay." Amazing how a couple words can carry so many meanings. "Archer, were you lovers?" I think I already knew the answer to that question, but I wanted to hear it from him.

"We were more than that."

"Oh, okay." Calm, Phoenix, be calm.

"We were..." He struggled to find the words. "More." Evidently, there weren't any. "But that is over now." He looked at me, his eyes were as hard as steel. "And it will never be again. You are my future. You are welcome here."

He turned back to the stone and raised his hand before it. I could feel the power rising in his body, I tried to pull my hand from his, but he held on tighter. As the power in him grew, he made circular motions in the air. Big sweeping, counter-clockwise circles. His arm moved faster and faster as a great rumbling started in the ground. I held onto Archer's hand with both of mine, prepared to jump out of the way of any boulders shaken loose by the great rumbling in the mountainside. Just when I thought the entire mountain was about to come down around me, the large circular stone moved.

Archer was straining with effort as the stone rolled slowly to the left. With his hand still in mine, he put his entire body into the action and was soon in a muscular lunge as he pushed the rock aside with his power. Power. His power. My brain suddenly put the pieces together. My power. He needed my power. I called to it. It woke quickly in my belly and flew down my arms and into Archer. His eyes widened as it hit him and he tried to keep it out.

"Let me help you," I called above the din as power backed up in my arms.

He grunted and shook his head.

"Archer, let me in!"

Something in him stilled. Without words he opened himself and my power flooded through him. He cried out as it shot through his body and out his arm. Our combined power hit the boulder with such force that it shot back like a marble flicked across the floor.

Archer dropped to his knees, and I released his hand. His breath was coming in ragged gulps. We both looked at the dark entryway the moving of the stone had revealed.

"I've never moved it that quickly." He stood shakily and took my hand again. "Thank you."

"You're welcome."

"Shall we go inside?" Although his legs shook, his voice was full of confidence and joy.

"Definitely."

We stepped into the passageway.

35

We walked hand in hand along the passage. It was dark, but I could feel smooth stone beneath my feet and lots of space around me. The ground felt like it was sloping gently upwards.

"Archer, are we going up?"

"Oh, yes, the lights."

It wasn't an answer to my question, but I didn't have to wait long to find one. Archer made this short hissing sound, and light started glowing from the floor. It formed a long thin line that stretched out before us. The light bled out towards the walls and encircled us in a ring of light that moved with us as we walked. This continued the entire length of the passage. Every step we took was fringed in a vertical halo of light.

We were indeed in a rising passageway, I could make out the change in elevation easily now. The ceiling had to be sixteen feet above us, and the width of the passage was about half that. Everywhere I looked was stone, but not the cruel stone of the tunnels I had stumbled upon, this was limestone, soft and welcoming to the eyes. It was the colour of sand, a calming beige with thin strips of copper and gold running through it. The sweeping passageway looked as if water had carved it.

"It's beautiful."

I didn't realize I'd stopped walking until Archer tugged on my hand. I tore my gaze from the curving walls and looked at him. He was smiling.

"Tip of the iceberg, babe," he quipped.

Archer pulled me forward, and I trotted eagerly behind him. The incline quickly grew steep. Super steep. The passage narrowed, and by the time we rounded a bend, things had gone vertical, and hand holds had appeared. There was no room to spread my wings, I would have to climb.

"Rock climbing?" I asked no one in particular.

"Is there a problem?" I looked up and saw Archer, cool as a cucumber, his spine straight, his chiselled body gleaming, framed by ambient light from the open space above him, each muscle standing in stark relief..... What was I complaining about again? Right, climbing, rock climbing.

"Seriously?" I sighed dramatically, grabbed the lowest hand hold and stepped onto the wall. "Seriously?"

"No one else has found it to be a problem."

We both knew that the 'no one' he was referring to was Mhyr. And damn it if jealousy doesn't get a girl moving. I tried to remember the brief instruction I'd had the one time I'd tried to climb a wall at a gym. The only thing I mined from my brain was the instructor with his backwards base-ball hat and artfully trimmed stubble, yelling 'use your legs' as I flailed in the ill-fitting harness. Sigh.

I was glad Archer had suggested a more rugged boot; they fit my feet snuggly, and the rubberized soles made clinging to the footholds slightly less frightening. I kept my attention on the next place to put my foot and then the next place to put my hand, never letting my mind wander to how high I had to climb or how far I had to fall. Archer was so silent as he moved up the wall that I couldn't tell where he was in space unless I looked right at him, and if I ran my eyes up or down the wall, I was sure I would fall. Did I mention I don't like rock climbing?

After a few minutes, my thighs were on fire, and my fingers were having trouble gripping the holds. I pushed off my right foot and stretched to reach the next hold, as my fingers touched it my foot slipped, and I screamed as I fell. As I fell my wings instinctively spread and smacked into the sides of the passage. It was painful, and I let out a second scream, sure now I would hit the ground with two broken wings.

Suddenly Archer's powerful hand wrapped around my wrist. I looked up to see him hanging down from the top of the wall. I grunted and threw up my left arm, which he caught easily.

"Damn it." My feet skidded along the wall as I searched for a foothold.

"You did very well."

My feet found holds, taking some weight off his arms.

"Do you want me to pull you up?" he asked, his voice studiously neutral.

"Let's do a half and half thing. I'll keep my feet on the wall, you pull."

"Excellent."

He started pulling, and I tried to keep up. He was so strong that he could have popped me like a cork out of that passage, but it probably would have dislocated both my shoulders. I was closer to the top of the wall than I had originally thought and within seconds Archer was pulling me onto a ledge. It was about three feet wide, and I knelt there as I looked around at his home.

"Holy shit."

We were in the peak of a mountain. The ceiling of the room, the very peak itself, rose to a point high above the centre of the room. Cream coloured stalactites hung there. The room was round and along the walls were arrow slits. They all started about a foot from the floor and rose up the wall to a height much taller than Archer.

"I'm glad you like it," Archer chuckled as he slipped off the ledge and landed softly on the floor five feet below.

Holy shit really was the best my mind could muster at that moment because about a dozen things happened at once. Okay, it was only two things, but it felt like a dozen. First, the beauty of the space threw me, and second, I had an overwhelming sense that I had been here before. Not only that I had been here, but that I knew this place intimately, almost as if I had lived here myself.

I crawled along the ledge that framed the deep hole I'd just climbed out of. Below me was a large mattress that was tucked partially under the lip of the ledge. I got to my feet and continued walking along to discover a living room type area with enormous beanbag chairs bunched haphazardly in piles. Completing the circle, I came to where Archer was standing before a large console. Screens showed various views of the valley and mountains surrounding his home. He touched a button, and with a soft grinding sound, the room began to spin.

But it wasn't the entire room. The ledge was stationary; it was the floor on which Archer stood that moved. The whole circular room surrounding the entrance swept gently to the right. I stood still as he drifted away, once again struck by the familiarity of the movement. I watched his hands on the console; he reached for a blue button, and before he pressed it, I knew that the walls of the room would spin. And they did, in the opposite direction from the console until an arrow slit was directly in front of Archer.

"The green button!" my voice rang out in the vast space.

Archer stilled, his back to me, his hand just above the green button. He looked like stone. After a few heartbeats, he reached out and touched the green button. The stone of the arrow slit before him opened like the petals of a flower. The green valley below was now visible.

"Have I been here before?" I asked.

"No."

I walked along the ledge towards him and sat down, letting my legs dangle over the side. The valley below was so green it was almost shocking against the soft beige of the limestone that framed it. I felt like I had been looking out at that valley for centuries.

"Why does this place feel so familiar?"

"It does?" Archer turned to me.

"Yes, I feel like I know the curves of the stone, the direction of the sun through the windows. You started the room turning, and it felt as natural as opening a door. How can that be?" I looked back at the entrance and said as an afterthought. "That was definitely not familiar though. I would have remembered that."

I felt Archer's hands on my thighs, he could move so fast.

"Phoenix, you've healed me."

"Twice."

"Yes, twice." he smiled, and my heart melted just a little. "My memories have bled into you."

"Because I healed you?"

"Yes," he took my hand in his and lifted it to his lips, running them lightly over my fingers. "Thank you."

My brain fought its way through my swirling hormones.

"Is that why the Guard doesn't want me healing creatures?"

His mouth stopped moving. He looked at me quizzically.

"Are you just figuring that out now?"

"Yes," I pulled my hand away. "I didn't know I was sucking memories out of people, the wings haven't shown me anything like that."

The words had no sooner left my mouth when I was hit with a memory. Suddenly I could see Mhyr naked above me. The roof was open, and stars shone behind her. I could feel her breath on my skin and her hair in my hands. The image was so strong I swayed backwards and would have fallen if Archer hadn't leapt onto the ledge and once again caught me.

"Are you all right?" He wrapped his arms around me.

"Ask, and ye shall receive."

"I'm sorry?" Archer asked gently.

"It's human speak," I rubbed at my eyes. "I saw a memory, your memory. You and Mhyr. Here."

"That was a long time ago," he murmured.

"I know, Archer." I reached out and touched his face. "I'm not worried about her."

"Good."

He hopped off the wall and reached out to me. He put his sturdy hands around my waist and lifted me easily from the wall. It's hard to make me feel delicate, but somehow he managed it.

"Memories are everything, Phoenix. They are our secrets, our power. You can heal any species in the pantheon of creatures that inhabit the Void. You could access their memories; learn their secrets." He looked at me seriously. "That is a very threatening power."

"I'd never thought about it that way."

"Well, get thinking about it. Fast. Because it is that power which has put you here."

"And where is here, exactly?" I said sarcastically. His tone was getting a bit strident for my liking.

"Here, Phoenix is about to enter one of the worst places in the Void to stop a madman and his army of thousands from tearing apart your soul."

I gulped audibly.

"Okay, now I'm scared."

"Then you are ready."

"Awesome."

And then a siren went off.

36

"What the hell!" I clamped my hands over my ears. Archer was at the controls in one quick leap. Instantly the siren cut off. "Is it Greldrom? Has he found me?"

"No, he does not know of my home."

"Then who is it?"

"Myhr."

I rushed to the console and looked out through the window. There, a stark slip of silver against the green of the valley was Myhr. You could tell by the black of her bra and long raven hair.

"This is bad," Archer said quietly.

"Why? She can't get in here, can she?"

"Yes, she can. And if she finds you here, it will not be pretty."

"Okay, we'll get into why she can just walk in here whenever she pleases, and why you're still scared of her another time. What do you we need to do now?"

"We need to get out of here." A beep sounded from the

console, and we both looked out the window. Myhr was now running up the scree-covered slope. "Fast."

I moved to the entrance, but Archer's hand on my shoulder stopped me.

"Over here."

Archer ran around to the opposite side of the room and began throwing pillows all over the place.

"What are you doing?" I asked.

"We need weapons." He had cleared the space of pillows and was now tossing the giant carpet that lay beneath them aside.

"I have a weapon," I responded.

"You need more."

With a quick flick of his wrist, he grabbed and twisted a small piece of metal embedded in the floor. A soft hiss filled the air as the stone floor lifted, and a large hatch opened at his feet.

"Come here."

Normally I don't enjoy being ordered around, but the contents of the hatch silenced me, and I moved to his side. The compartment was full of weapons. Long swords, short blades, clubs, throwing stars, spiked balls on rusty chains. Each one had a fine layer of dust on it, but their disuse did nothing to quell my shock. This was the stronghold of a man who knew incredible violence. This was a side of Archer I did not know.

"Arms out, stay still."

I spread my arms and Archer went to work. With a practised ease he slipped short, slim blades sheathed in thick leather onto my arms. The blades fit perfectly along the length of my forearms; he wrapped thin leather straps around my arms to hold them in place; they felt comfortable. They felt right. As I marvelled at this, Archer made quick work of strapping two swords to his back and a throwing blade to each shin.

Now sufficiently suited up for battle, Archer grabbed my hand and pulled me towards the ledge. Before I could say 'how do we climb down,' he tossed me onto the ledge and vaulted up beside me. Then, like some kind of superhuman Tarzan, he wrapped an arm around my waist and jumped into the blackness of the entranceway.

We plummeted several feet before his free hand grabbed hold of the wall and we jolted to a stop. I did my best to keep my wings close to my body as Archer swung and jumped from the wall to catch a hold lower down. With every jump, my stomach shot up into my throat. I clung to Archer's shoulders and tried not to scream. I only whimpered twice, I swear.

I thought he'd put me down when we reached the ground, but he kept his arm tight around my waist and ran full tilt down the hall. I was feeling like Fay Wray in King Kong.

"Archer put me down."

"No time." His voice came out clear for someone running full tilt while carrying me. "We have to get to the other side of the mountain and off the rocks before we can travel. Hang on."

We were at the boulder-covered doorway. Without missing a step, he twisted me around his body, so I was on his back. I wrapped my legs around his waist and held onto his shoulders, keeping my head close to his back. The boulder practically exploded out of the doorway. I guess it was easier going out than coming in. Archer made a sharp move to the left and started scaling the rock face.

"Holy shit, you're strong!" I shouted.

Archer grunted and kept climbing. We were moving up

and sideways, and he was covering major ground. The mountain was enormous, but Archer was strong. He scaled a third of the way around and then dropped to a path below. The path was narrow but unobstructed, letting him run full out with me on his back.

Up ahead, rocks flowed down the mountainside. They were quickly filling the path.

"She knows what we're doing. Hold on!" He shouted and picked up speed. I looked left and saw a large boulder bearing down on us. Archer kept running, and the boulder kept coming.

"Archer!" I screamed.

The boulder hit the path in front of us. With a shout and a call of power, Archer stepped up the side of the passage and leapt into the air. He was trying to jump the boulder, but when my wings felt the air beneath them, they spread out behind me. I whispered in Archer's ear.

"It's my turn."

My wings were strong and eager as they pulled us higher into the sky. Archer reached up and wrapped his arms around mine, strengthening our hold. I flew high over the rocky pathways, and soon we were out over the mountain's slope.

"There she is," he said, his voice even and cold.

I chanced a look back and saw Mhyr standing at the mountain's edge with hate in her eyes. She locked eyes with me and then, guessing our plan, practically threw herself down the slope.

"What is her problem!?" I bellowed into the wind, dropping into a dive.

The wind cut at our faces as I flew as fast as I could to the green valley below.

A little too fast. We were going to crash.

"Shit!" I screamed.

"Tuck and roll," Archer said calmly.

I had just enough time to figure out what he was talking about, draw in my wings and mould myself to his body. He pulled our bodies into a ball, and we somersaulted across the grass, my body stuck to his like glue.

We rolled once, twice, and on the third, we Travelled.

37

A rcher must be some kind of Travelling wizard because we were through the Time Tunnel instantly. It was amazing. No weird lights, screaming wind or long minutes glued to his body... Okay, it had a downside.

We hit the ground hard and kept rolling. I got flashes of sandy ground and a jet black sky as we somersaulted before Archer unfurled his body and vaulted me into the air. My wings opened, and I brought myself softly to the ground with my feet planted squarely. Archer was by my side as I touched down. He gestured at me to be silent and took my hand. I followed him at a jog into a nearby rocky inlet.

"Why are we back on the mountain?" I whispered. He didn't answer me. "Ar.."

"No." His hand covered my mouth, his voice was barely audible. "No names here. We are not back on the mountain. We are near the mouth of the City of Caves. Take in your surroundings before judging them." He moved forward between the rocks. "And tuck in those wings or they will spot us."

I chewed back the many unsaid words trying to escape my mouth and did as I was told. I also vowed that I would learn as much as I could about the ways of the Void, and how to fight, so I would never have to take orders from him again. It's good to have goals.

I looked at the surrounding stone. This was not the cold grey of the mountainside or the light lime of its interior. This rock held a multitude of deep orange stripes and yellowing beige ribbons. We were in a deep, narrow cavern with the sensual curves that only years of flowing water can form. It was freezing, and I was glad for the thick leather covering my torso. The short blades on my forearms were a comforting weight.

Up the path, Archer crouched behind a boulder; I jogged over and hunkered down beside him. He pointed at an area to the left of the rock and then sat back on his heels so I could crawl in front and look. Evidently, Archer wasn't used to a girlfriend with wings because he didn't leave me enough room and was knocked backwards as I moved around the boulder. He grunted heavily as he fell back onto his ass and I was glad it was too dark for him to see the smile on my face.

I kept low and peeked around the rock. We were maybe fifteen feet above a large sandy clearing. A crumbling set of carved stone steps descended before us. Walls of rock that reached high into the sky surrounded the clearing. I could see that there were carvings on these walls, but from our hiding place I couldn't make them out. In the distance, maybe a hundred paces away, was the entrance to the City of Caves.

There was no mistaking it. The doorway itself was a rectangular hole that looked like it had been fashioned by heating the rock until it was as soft as taffy and then stretching it apart. The edges smooth and pulled back like the skin of an animal that had been recently butchered. The stone looked as shiny as raw meat in the firelight.

There was a lot of fire here.

Above the opening was a lantern that threw long licks of fire up into the sky. Two tall torches, with equally violent flames, joined it on either side of the entryway. On the ground before the entrance was a large fire pit. The flames here were tinged with blue and were being stoked by a very muscular minion with a very weighty spear.

"Blue flame?" shouted a voice emerging from the entrance. It belonged to an equally muscular minion who was dragging a mace beside him. "Why didn't you sound the alarm?"

"Alarm?" I whispered, and Archer was instantly beside me. We moulded ourselves to the rock and kept listening.

"Bah!" replied the minion with the spear. "It's barely blue, probably an animal or two roaming through the rocks." The other minion had joined him at the fire. "Could be a nice bit of sport for us, eh?"

"Could be..." the minion with the mace didn't sound convinced.

"Relax Yagak. In all our time at these gates, we've never caught more than a coyote." Spear minion pulled a flask from somewhere and took a long drink before passing it to his friend. "Have a drink." He burped, loudly. "Go on."

"You're right, Jogug." He took the flask. "And when you're right, you're right." He took a deep drink and passed it back. "What we need is a night off to go hunting. To really let our hair down."

They laughed heartily.

"You've watched too many humans!" Jogug said between bouts of laughter.

"I sure have," Yagak replied, equally jovial, "But they're so pink, how can I resist?"

This elicited more laughter from the pair, and they passed the flask back and forth again. Archer nodded over his shoulder, and we moved back from the rock.

"How are we going to get past them?" His voice held the tone of someone thinking out loud.

"That's potent stuff," I said. We could hear the minions' laughter growing louder. "It should help us out."

"How so?" Archer's attention had snapped back to me with an almost physical intensity.

"Well, it'll slow them down. Make them less responsive." A plan was forming as I spoke. "We just need them to get a little drunker and then we sweep down fast and take them out."

"A blitz attack," he mused.

"It could work."

"I think it is the best chance we have," he agreed. "How quickly can you get down there?"

"I don't know, those stairs don't look very safe, and I'm not great with running."

"Stop forgetting your wings," Archer grumbled.

"Oh!" I looked over my shoulder at them. Their colours were pale in the semi-darkness. "Why do I keep doing that?"

"I don't know," he replied dryly.

"It was a rhetorical question, thank you," I snapped back. Archer leant forward and kissed me on the mouth.

"I'm sorry," he murmured.

"Thank you," I whispered. I pulled back from him and as if with one mind, our game faces snapped into place. "I can be at the entrance in three seconds."

"Good," he replied.

Archer crawled back down the path and into the deeper

shadows, I followed him. Once we were in complete darkness, we got to our feet and, as he talked, we checked our weapons were secure. I also made sure the straps of my top were tied tightly. I really didn't need a wardrobe malfunction in a black pit of bloodthirsty minions.

"You will leap off the rock and into the air. It will draw their attention. Go high, it will pull them together and away from the door, then dive down on them, fast. I will sprint around behind them and break their necks before you touch the ground." He stopped messing with his weapons and looked at me. "Don't worry." He smiled. "You'll get to kill plenty of things inside."

"That's what I'm afraid of," I mumbled, which is hard to do when you're already whispering.

"On three," he said.

"Yep," I turned towards the dark open space at the end of the path.

"One."

Oh, man.

"Two."

Am I really doing this?

"Three."

38

I sprinted down the path and with a short flap of my wings jumped onto a boulder and then leapt into the air.

The icy night air coated my body, and without instruction, my wings spread and drew me higher into the sky. I heard the minions below cry out, and the sound of two pairs of tiny stomping feet met my ears. As I soared to the centre of the clearing, I looked down and saw that our plan was working. The minions were in front of the fire and moving drunkenly towards me, their weapons raised but unsteady. I hovered in the air above them.

"Get down, you freak!" Yagak yelled, brandishing his mace.

"Yeah!" joined Jogug. "Come down and fight!"

Jogug's spear pointed wildly as he stumbled around. He attempted to jab the air, stumbled, did a pirouette, and smacked Yagak on the ass with it. Yagak bellowed, throwing his arms into the air. This caused his mace to swing around and smack Jogug in the face. Jogug dropped to the ground like a stone and slumped over his spear, which was sticking up towards Yagak, who turned and yelled at the sight of his fallen comrade, throwing his arms in the air again, which set the mace swinging again. It shot up and back in an arch, smacking him in the head. Knocked out cold, he fell forward, impaling himself on the spear.

"Wow," I whispered.

I flew down to the minions and took a closer look. Neither was breathing.

"Wow." I shook my head at the two creatures; dark fluid was oozing from their many wounds.

"What happened?" Archer was at my side.

"I should be asking you that. Where were you?"

"I fell down the stairs." He said the words quickly, and I had to ask him to repeat himself. He sighed and then hung his head slightly. "I fell down the stairs."

"Really?" I stretched out the word and let my smugness saturate every syllable.

"Aren't you going to ask if I'm okay?" he asked, his tone pouty.

"Are you okay?"

"Yes," he said grimly. He turned back to the minions. "Now, what happened to them?"

"Well, the first one accidentally smacked the second one who accidentally smacked him back, killing him, and then he accidentally smacked himself which made him fall forward onto the spear, killing himself." I sighed heavily. "It was like a macabre version of Dumb and Dumber."

"I will assume that is a human thing and ignore it."

I rolled my eyes. Archer squared his shoulders and looked at the entrance to the caves. In the firelight his eyes were piercing silver. His gaze remained steadily focused on the dark entrance as he spoke.

"It is time. You must keep your wits about you. What you

see in there," Archer's voice faltered slightly. "What you see me do will change you. I will do my best to save your hands from shedding blood."

I cut him off.

"I asked you here, ah..." I almost said his name but stopped the word. "I take the risk knowingly." I took his hand in mine. His eyes never strayed from the gate, but he squeezed my hand tightly. "I am so glad you are here to help me. Thank you."

Sadness flitted across his face.

"You must stay close to me." He turned to me. "Promise me."

"I promise."

That word held so much power here. Like an invisible thread, power wove its way through my body, across the space between us and into Archer. I felt it entwine itself around his heart, binding him to me. Archer shivered.

"Then let us go."

He dropped my hand and sprinted for the entrance to the caves.

39

Although the night sky was bright with stars and torches burned brightly either side of the entrance, the second we passed through the giant stone arch all light vanished. I turned swiftly on my heel to look back towards the entrance and saw only inky blackness.

"Shit," I said.

Archer was beside me, his voice low as he spoke, his face inches from my ear.

"It is their way."

"But I can't frigging see!" I said, not hiding the panic creeping into my voice.

"Open your mind. Use your power to see."

"How?" I was starting to feel desperate.

"First," he took my hand in the dark. "Breathe."

I hadn't realised I was holding my breath. Most people hyperventilate when they're scared. Not me. I just hold my breath until I pass out. I took a deep breath and let it out as slowly as I could. It wasn't quite yoga class slow, but it was definitely helping. After a few deep breaths, Archer spoke.

"Good." He squeezed my hand. "Now open the part of you that can see the portals."

"But how do I...." Archer cut me off.

"Just make the request of your power, trust yourself."

"Okay."

I let out yet another deep, slow breath and focused my intention on the centre of my body, where my power lived. I couldn't tell in the all-consuming darkness if I'd closed my eyes, but it didn't matter, the power in me responded to my call and began to stretch and fill my body.

"Good."

Archer breathed the word against my neck and the power in me pulsed more strongly. I called out to it with a single word; sight. I asked it of myself and the strange and wonderful energies that moved through me, and as the word tumbled through my mind, the pieces of me became one.

My eyes had been open.

The first thing I saw was the silver of Archer's bare chest, it gleamed. Everything moved before me in a grey scale with shimmers of colour that clung to different parts of him. The place where his ribs could be removed, his hands, the sword at his back, they all shimmered with a deep purple aura. Gradually my normal sight took over, the blackness of the tunnel disappeared, and I could see the torches that lined the walls, the icy grey stone that they had carved the tunnel into. I looked into Archer's face and watched a grim smile flit across it.

"A spell?" I asked. He answered with a brief nod.

"We must get moving."

I kept close to him as we proceeded down the rough stone passage. The walls and floor were moist. There must be a major water source down here, I thought. Even with the spell lifted the place was still dark; torches were spaced along the wall at intervals just wide enough to make shadowy moments between them.

We continued in silence. Archer's arms were loose at his sides, belying the tension I felt radiating from him. His swords hung crossed on his back, their hilts gleamed in the torchlight and in the silence of the passage, I could almost hear them singing to be set free. My own hands were like rigid claws at my sides. My sword was hidden behind my hair, and my wings were tucked tightly to my body like a dog with its tail between its legs. This place terrified me. It was quiet, too quiet. I had heard mention of such terrible things here, and yet there was nothing but a seemingly unending passage that snaked deeper into the earth. I called out to Archer in a harsh whisper.

"Hey!"

He kept walking. I raced forwarded and grabbed his shoulder.

"Hey!"

It happened so quickly I thought I'd dreamt it. One second my hand was on Archer's shoulder, the next he pinned me to the wall, his silver hand around my throat.

"What the f..." I choked out. His hand spasmcd around my neck and then released me. I slid to the ground and my wings wrapped around me as I rubbed my throat.

"I'm so sorry," Archer was against the opposite wall, breathing very hard. "I told you this place would bring out another side of me."

"Oh yeah, blame the victim," I said with venom. Apparently, this was another mistake on my part.

"This place is evil!" Archer pulled apart my wings and was inches from my face. His normally tranquil silver eyes had turned a dark black. I stayed perfectly still as he spoke.

"Can't you feel it?" He sniffed the air. "It smells like blood." He moved back from me. "I should never have come here."

I spoke as calmly as I could.

"You don't have to stay."

Although the prospect of being alone in these tunnels scared the crap out of me, Archer's reaction scared me even more. I did not need him freaking out on me when the fighting started.

"You don't feel it?" His voice sounded far away, and his eyes were still black.

"Feel what, babe?"

"The evil."

He closed his eyes and began taking deep, slow breaths.

Oh, this is going swimmingly, I thought to myself. I'm inside one of the worst places in the Void, and my boyfriend is having some sort of Vietnam flashback.

Keeping my breathing as even as possible, I looked up and down the passage. I could see nothing particularly evil about the space; there were no ominous stains on the ground, or body parts stapled to the walls. It was just a rough stone passage.

"Why can't I feel it?"

"You have little knowledge of evil, bird girl," Archer's voice was like acid. "Your heart does not know violence like the rest of us. You are too shielded, too pure." He chuckled. He was really going to lose it, like any second now.

"Then I'll try, babe," I said in my most soothing, non-confrontational voice. Yes, I have one of those. "I'll open my heart and try."

Archer's response was to languidly draw a sword from the sheath at his spine and lay it on the ground next to him. Oh, shit.

With fear now singing through my veins, I willed my

heart to open. I closed my eyes and reached deep into myself and opened my heart to the world around me.

The evil was waiting for me.

It ripped through my soul like a scream. My body twisted where I sat as evil, pure unadulterated evil, coursed through me. I shoved a fist in my mouth to stifle my cries as centuries of pain and obscene acts flitted through my mind's eye. I could see the orgies of blood and flesh, the mingling of bodies and skin, the rage and the perversity that coated this place. The residue may not have been visible to my naked eyes, but my heart unshielded could not ignore it.

Panting, I turned my thoughts to myself; I drew my wings around me and rebuilt the shields around my heart, layering them with my power, a power pure and free of evil and of darkness. My power, the power from my wings, from my heart, a power that coursed through me undiluted.

I was on my hands and knees when I came back to my senses. My wings hummed with energy, my limbs sang with power. I had wanted to destroy Greldrom for my own needs, but now, now I knew he had to die. For the good of the Void, he had to die. This madness had to stop.

"Now you see." Archer was kneeling beside me. I looked into his eyes, they were still black. Still covered in a sheen of sweat, he looked more in control.

"He has to die," I said, my voice steady, but grim.

"Yes."

"Tonight."

"Yes."

We held each other's gaze, light and dark, each struggling to understand the other, each wanting the other free from pain. I went to him and he wrapped his arms around me as our lips met.

"Now isn't this cozy!" a voice cackled.

40

A group of five minions were coming up the passage. The one in front had a mace in its hand.

"Our leader will be most pleased! Extra flesh for us tonight, boys!"

All but one minion cheered as the leader looked over his shoulder at them. It's a bad idea to turn your back when dealing with The Archer and a Phoenix.

Before he could complete the turn of his head, Archer had driven his sword through the creature's gut. The minion let out a little sigh and then shook as Archer dragged his blade up through its body, practically cutting it in half. Bright green blood sprayed the corridor. The others screamed, and Archer had two more cut down before they could move. Purple and black fluids joined the mess.

By this time I had recovered from the shock of seeing a minion hacked in half and could move again. With the help of my wings, I shot forward and grabbed one of the two remaining minions, the one that hadn't joined in cheering with the others. The second minion turned tail and ran down the passage at breakneck speed. Archer went after it. I cried out to him as he disappeared around a bend. I waited, my breath held, but he did not come back.

I looked around me, multicoloured fluid and minion parts were everywhere. Archer had done all this in seconds. Crazy. I heard a soft moan and remembered I was holding on to a minion. It was smaller than the others and looked up at me with frightened watery eyes. Its face was covered in splatters of green, purple and black. It choked on phlegm as it tried to speak.

"Please, don't kill me."

I sighed heavily; I really didn't need a moral dilemma this early in the evening.

"Then you're coming with me."

I looked around and pulled a blood-soaked rag off one of the bodies. I took the cloth and tied the minion's hands and moved it into a sitting position. The minion started to cry. I was losing time. Archer could be anywhere by now.

"Please stop crying," I begged it. "I'm not going to hurt you."

"They were my brothers."

What could I say to that? We are all somebody's something. And here in the belly of the beast, there was no time to acknowledge such things.

"I'm not going to hurt you," I repeated, "As long as you help me."

"Help you?" Tears moved silently down his face.

"Yes, help me. I need to get to the throne room, and you are going to take me there."

"Then kill me now, for they will destroy me when we get there."

"Come on, man! I don't have time for this!" Power flared inside me. "I am here to destroy Greldrom and put an end to this terrible place!"

"You are? Truly?"

"Truly." I placed a hand on the creature's shoulder, and as I let my power flow into him, formal words fell from my mouth. "Renounce this evil and help me to the throne room, and I will see that you live."

"I renounced it some time ago, Lady. I will do whatever I can to help you end this terrible place."

I could taste the truth in his words. Even in the darkest corners of Time goodness can be found. I untied his hands, and as he rubbed at his wrists, I plucked a feather from my wing. The creature looked up at me, astonished. I placed my left hand under his chin and with my right used the feather to wipe his brothers' blood from his face.

"What is your name?"

"Spin, my lady. Spin."

The magic within the feather made quick work of cleaning his blood-smeared face. I shook the feather, and the blood flew from it. I handed the gleaming feather to Spin. He took it reverently and tucked it into the band of his loincloth.

"Ok, Spin, show me to the throne room."

He smiled and took my hand.

41

Walking hand in hand with a minion is not comfortable. The height difference, the scaly palms, the weird way they walk, the phlegm, the list goes on. I went with the height difference when I told him it wasn't working, and Spin accepted that happily. He was so trusting; he kept looking up at me with his big, round eyes and an enormous smile. It would have been cute if I wasn't in the City of Caves with no idea where Archer was or what I would find around the next bend.

"Okay, Spin, talk to me."

"I am so glad you have come! For too long now we minions have been forced to do terrible things under the guidance of our leader."

"Yes, Spin, we can talk about that stuff later. Now I need to know all about these caves. The layout, the dangers. We've been on the same path for a very long time, what gives?" I had decided not to find Archer. He had proven himself to be an accomplished killing machine and until I stopped Greldrom this place would be very dangerous for both of us. I had to make finding, and gulp, killing Greldrom my priority.

"Oh," Spin stopped walking. "You want to take a different path?" He looked confused.

"I don't know, do I?"

"You said to take you to the throne room; this is the fastest way to the throne room."

"You mean this path just goes straight to the heart of the city?"

"Yes," he said proudly.

Oh double crap, did this mean Archer was up ahead running right into the lion's den? I needed to get out of this passage. There had to be another way through this place, but how? The walls were seamless stone as far as I could see.

"Spin, I can't just walk straight in, I need to get there without being seen." He looked confused, so I spelt it out for him. "We need to go a secret way."

"Oooohhh, the Secret Way," he said with a knowing nod. "I see. Follow me."

He continued down the passage; I was about to remind him I needed to get off the main path and that it was a miracle we had met no other minions when he put his hand on the wall and hummed a little tune. It was just three notes, do re mi or something like that, and a fissure appeared in the rock.

"Follow me, my lady," he said with a smile and disappeared into the crack.

It was a minion sized crack. I was pretty sure I could get through the hole itself, but if the passage remained that size, we had a problem. I put my head into the hole and called out to Spin.

"Um, Spin?"

"Yes, my lady," the rock slightly muffled his voice.

"I'm not sure I will fit in there. I think I can get through this crack, but..."

"Do not worry, the path is large once you are through," he called cheerily from behind the rock.

"Ok," I said under my breath.

I backed up a bit and looked at the hole. I would need to get down low to get my wings through unscathed. Basically, I would have to slither through on my belly. I exhaled; the minion blood that had soaked my pants hadn't yet dried and would absorb every molecule of crud I came in contact with as I snaked through this hole. I would be so filthy when this was over. I was about to complain to Spin again when my wings tugged at my back reminding me why I was here. Get over yourself, Phoenix, I scolded silently and put my head into the hole.

The passage on the other side was large enough. It wasn't as full or well excavated as the main path and what little light there was came from randomly placed torches, but it would do. I stayed close to Spin as we moved along, which wasn't difficult. He seemed very reluctant to go forward. After the third time I'd walked into him, I stopped and crouched down to talk to him.

"What's the problem?"

"Problem? No, problem." He smiled, and even in the dim light, it looked tense and scared.

"Really? You seem very frightened, Spin." I put a hand on his shoulder, a little dribble of power flared between us, and he shrugged off my hand.

"Not here!" he whispered, looking frantically up and down the path. "This is a very dark path, very dark. We could meet wicked creatures here, villainous."

"I thought you said this was the secret way?" I asked, my

right hand casually resting on the blade Archer had strapped to my left forearm.

"Secret to most, not all," Spin replied. "There are no true Secrets here, my lady." The word secret had a weight to it as it left his mouth.

"I will protect us," I said, trying to reassure the little guy. "Lead the way."

"You may have to fight," he said, a slight quiver in his voice.

I straightened up and pulled out the short blade I had been caressing.

"I figured."

42

We moved forward through the tunnel. I kept one hand lightly skimming the stone wall to my left, my right arm out before me, blade in hand. Spin was practically wrapped around my legs.

"Spin?" My voice was barely a whisper, he was so close that hearing me was not an issue.

"Yes, my lady?"

"Is this another one of those secret door tunnels? Could someone come leaping out at us through the walls?"

"Yes, my lady."

"Oh, joy." The sarcasm was obvious even in a whisper.

"Yes, my lady."

Man, he sounded so much like Sid it made my heart hurt. Except Sid would never have cowered at my feet. Sid would have been charging ahead, ready to strike down whoever crossed our paths. I needed Sid now. A crazy thought popped into my head. Crazy. And exciting, very exciting. I tried to keep myself in check as I asked Spin my crazy question.

"Do you know all the minions here?"

"No, my lady, there are too many of us."

"That's comforting."

"Sarcasm, my lady?"

"Yep."

"Did you learn that in your world, my lady?"

"Yep."

"I see," he replied, his little forehead creased with thought.

"You may not know everyone here, but would you be able to find someone?" Spin looked puzzled. "If I told you their name, would you be able to find them? Is there like a main hive brain thing you could tap into?"

"Hive brain?" The question was genuine, Spin was far too innocent to be condescending.

"A place where information is stored about all of you minions. Where you live, where you could be in this massive place."

"Who are you looking for?"

His voice had turned dark. I stopped walking and discovered he was several paces behind me.

"Who are you looking for, my lady?" He drifted towards me, apprehension on his face. "I am taking you to the heart of this evil place, to the very throne of our leader. Who else could you possibly be looking for here?"

"Sid." Unexpected tears welled up as my voice caught in my throat. "I'd like to see Sid."

Spin stood in that dark, cold, wet, scary, stone passageway and looked at me. I could see bad news coming my way from behind his eyes. I told my heart to be strong. I told myself that no matter what he said, I would complete this mission, find Archer and then get us the hell out of here. Spin opened his mouth to speak, and I felt the blood drain from my face.

"I know the minion named Sid, and I know where he is." Spin stopped talking and looked at the floor.

"Where is he, Spin? Tell me."

"He is in the throne room, my lady." He looked me in the eyes. "He is strung up in the throne room."

43

———————

"Asshole!" My world swam red. My wings unfurled, knocking a flaming torch from the wall. The flame guttered, plunging us into shadow. I continued ranting to the air. "If he thought I was going to kill him before, I am going to double kill that bastard now!"

"Lady, calm yourself, please!"

Spin was hopping around at my feet as I strutted down the corridor. I unfurled my wings as much as the passage would allow and I took out every torch we passed. I didn't care. Their puny flames couldn't hurt me.

"He's torturing him, isn't he?"

"Yes." Spin was trying to speak as he coughed and sputtered beside me.

"And everybody gets to watch, don't they?"

"Yes."

"How long?"

"My lady?"

I halted and dropped to my knees, my angry faces inches from Spin's.

"How long has this been going on?" I asked through gritted teeth.

"We- we- we have no concept of Time here, my lady," Spin stammered, "You ask how long and I cannot answer."

"Damn it!" I was back on my feet.

"But why, my lady," Spin's voice was stronger now, "Why care so much for this one? Why let only his pain matter? He is not the first!" I stopped walking but did not turn around. "How do you think the City of Caves got its reputation? How do you think these walls became so coated with evil and fear? Your friend Sid is no greater than the multitudes that have hung from those walls. Be angry for all of them," he laid a gentle hand on my calf, "For all of us."

As his tiny hand touched me a vision screamed through my body. I could see a room garishly lit by many, many torches. The air was thick with soot and heat from the flames. The smell of sweat and putrid things coated my tongue. Greldrom sat on a pile of bones raised high above the room on a plinth of stone. Minions rolled on the filth-covered floor at his feet. Some laughed, drunk or high, others fought with fists and blades. I saw one minion grab another and roughly hack the ear from its head. He tossed the ear into the crowd; another minion grabbed it and tore it apart with its teeth, gulping it down greedily.

Minions hung from the walls, splayed out by chains that pulled at their wrists and ankles, their bodies stretched to impossible angles. The minion to my left was dead. Its belly was bloated, and its tongue hung grey and dry from its mouth. To my right, a minion screamed. His mind had gone, and although he screamed and screamed, it was barely audible above the din in the low-ceilinged room. I hung there as quietly as I could. I was here for sport. Here because my brothers thought it would be funny to have the little one on the wall for a time. So far I had avoided more than a whipping, and I hoped that if I remained quiet, soon they would tire of me and let me down. It was then that Greldrom spoke.

"Silence!" The hall was immediately quiet. Even the screaming mess beside me had closed his mouth. "What have we here?" He was looking right at me. Evil dripped from his words. "Who tied this little present to the wall?"

He stood and walked towards me. My bowels loosened.

"No!" I cried.

Power shot through my body, breaking the vision. I found myself on my hands and knees, Spin a few feet away. When he touched me, I had become him. Absorbed by his memory, I experienced it all as he had done. My god, it was horrible. The fear. The violence. The cannibalism. I moved to the edge of the passage and vomited. Spin's voice was clear and cold as it filled the passage.

"I am glad you stopped that when you did, my lady. I did not wish to see more."

"I'm sorry," I wiped at my mouth as best I could with my shaky hands. "That's never happened before." I sat back against the wall, edging away from the small pool of vomit. "I'm sorry you had to relive that," I spat out a last mouthful of bile. "I'm sorry it happened to you."

"Thank you, lady. It was quite some time ago." He smiled grimly. "Besides, you stopped the vision before the nasty stuff started."

"Holy crap, Spin. That wasn't the nasty stuff?"

"Not even half of it, my lady."

"Shit."

"Yes, that about sums it up," he laughed dryly.

"Spin?"

"Yes, my lady."

"Let's go get this bastard."

"I'd like that."

44

———————

We continued down the passage, making impressive time. Towards what, I didn't really know, but we were making great time doing it. Spin seemed bolstered by our vision experience. I think having someone witness and validate his pain helped him feel less victimized. I was glad for him and happy that I now knew what I was walking into, but could have done without the taste of vomit that still lingered on my tongue and the rolling emptiness in my belly. Note to self, never Travel without a water bottle and a power bar.

"We're almost there!" Spin whispered beside me.

"Good."

We slowed our pace. As we had walked, Spin had filled me in on the layout of the throne room. We would arrive at a fissure in the rock near the ceiling of the hall. From our vantage point, we could observe the entire throne room and plan our next move.

"Around the next bend, my lady."

We were moving towards a wall of sound comprising snorting, coughing, raucous laughter, shouting and the unmistakable sound of flesh hitting flesh, hard. My steps slowed.

"How many will be in there?" I asked Spin.

Adrenaline was slowly starting to flood my veins. Spin was so close to me his head kept bouncing into my thigh as we walked.

"Hard to say. A hundred, maybe two. More, if Greldrom has called them."

"Called them?"

"As our leader, he can use his power to call us to him. It is how he draws us to battle, or for his amusements."

"Wouldn't you have felt it if he had?" I asked.

"I don't think so, my lady. Your aura is strong, it may be shielding me."

"I can do that?" There was so much I still didn't know about being a Traveller.

"Yes, my lady. You are powerful." He smiled up at me, I couldn't help but return his grin.

"Aw shucks," I giggled. Spin abruptly stopped.

"We are here."

My body snapped to attention, my wings folded tight to my back and a small current of power, like a tiny bolt of lightning, shivered through my body. I became eerily calm. My breathing was deep and full, I could feel my ribs moving with every breath as my blood flowed smoothly through my veins. Spin had pointed to a deep crack in the rocky side of the path. A red glow poured through the crack and spilt into the passage. I walked towards it, Spin close at my heels.

"Watch our backs."

I felt Spin turn, putting his back to me as he scanned the corridor, making sure no one snuck up on us. I knelt in front of the fissure and looked down into the throne room.

Minions were everywhere. There must have been three

hundred of them; they seemed to roll over each other like a boiling mass of grey flesh. The sides of the room were fringed with piles of rubble. Minions climbed up and down, some of their own accord, others tossed, their bodies dashed against the jagged rock. They passed bottles full of black liquid from hand to hand. Fire pits were placed throughout the room, each one roasting some kind of flesh over the flames. In another area, a ring of minions had formed, and at its centre, two creatures fought with blades. Both dripped with bright green blood. Some sort of orgy was taking place on the ground directly below me, although it looked no less violent than the rest of the room.

Like in Spin's vision, minions hung limply from chains on the wall, their bodies emaciated and bruised. I scanned the line of splayed bodies and there, closest to Greldrom's throne, was Sid. My Sid. The once noble creature who had been my friend for years, who had brought me into this fantastic world and to my true self, was chained naked to the wall.

He hung by his wrists, his legs hanging limply below him. His eyes were closed, and his head rested heavily on his right shoulder, his tongue a protruding grey mass. A dark stain spread down the wall below him. Further marks of trauma crisscrossed his body. It was terrible. Even though he had betrayed me, I couldn't bare seeing him like this. Refusing to let my tears surface, I scanned the room again, planning my entrance. These bastards were going to pay.

But as my eyes roamed over the room, I realised that not all the minions were willingly taking part. Some had the same frightened look on their face that Spin did. Some looked like they wished for nothing more than to blend into the walls and leave this terrible place. But some were definitely enjoying themselves, enjoying themselves very much. The play of bully and victim was everywhere.

In the centre of all this was Greldrom. His throne was just as I had seen it in Spin's mind. He sat on his dais atop a pile of bones, a look of pure delight painted on his ugly face. A small minion was at his side holding out a colossal piece of meat which Greldrom periodically gnawed on. A second minion was at his other side with a bottle of the dark liquid.

"Spin," I whispered. He was instantly by my side.

"Yes, my lady."

"What is that they're drinking?"

He peered into the room.

"Minion poison."

"What?"

"The black drink. It makes us do terrible things. Makes minions forget themselves and do his bidding without question."

"But Big G is drinking it too?"

"Big G?"

"Greldrom."

"Ah, that is funny." He didn't laugh but stared at Greldrom with hate in his eyes. "It is his poison, my lady."

"Spin, I probably know the answer to this, but," I looked down at the multitude of minions. "Is that a lot of minions?"

"That's a lot of minions."

"Is that all the minions?"

"Well, almost, there would be a few left to guard the entrance to the city."

"They're dead."

"Oh, then that is probably everyone."

"Right, right..." I nodded my head to no one in particular.

Spin let out a strange grunt. I turned towards him and

time slowed down. A long gash had appeared across his throat, purple blood poured down his chest. Two burly minions were behind him, one held a short blade that dripped with Spin's blood, the other was lunging towards me. With absolute silence and savagery, my right hand shot forward and grasped the minion by his neck. Power flared through my hand and with superhuman strength, Traveller strength, I felt myself crushing his windpipe, turning it to pulp in my hand. Simultaneously, my left hand tore free the blade tied to my right forearm and flung it at the second minion. It pierced his belly, and before he could scream, I was on him.

Still holding the other minion by the throat, I drew the blade roughly up through the chest cavity of the second minion. Green blood sprayed my face and body as I pulled the blade higher and higher. I could feel the evil of the place seeping into me, and I used its power to pull the blade up through the creature's skull until pieces of the minion's brain fell to the ground. I threw the now dead body of the other minion on top of the dissected carcass. Its neck was a fleshy mass, the head hung at an odd angle.

The evil pulsed stronger in my veins and I raised the green soaked blade to my mouth. Slowly, ever so slowly, I brought it closer. Inches from my mouth, my hungry tongue reached for the blade. As the bright green blood was about to touch my tongue, a voice filled the passage. It was a weak voice, filled with pain and fear, it was the voice of a soul splayed open, and it called to the deepest part of me. It called to my heart, and my power responded, shedding the evil of the place and bringing me back to myself.

"No, my lady, please, no."

I dropped the blade and rushed to Spin's side. The cut in his neck was shallow but had cut through something important. His chest was a wet purple mess, his face was splattered with the bright fluid.

"Oh, Spin, I'm sorry, I'm so so sorry." Tears were flowing down my cheeks as I tried desperately to hold the wound together.

"Help me..." His voice was so weak, I could feel his pulse slowing under my hands.

"I'm sorry, Spin, I'm so sorry."

I put my forehead to his and cried. Tears dripped from my eyes and fell on his face. Where they touched his skin, the purple instantly vanished, little dots and streaks of clean flesh appeared. My tears continued down over his chin, and as they touched the wound, a tingling started in my hands. Startled, I sat back on my heels and looked down at Spin. Could I do it? Could I heal him? I know I healed Archer after I drove the baseball bat through his belly, but our connection had bolstered me. The vision I had of healing him in the past told me I could do it again. But could I heal Spin? Could I heal a creature I had never met before? That I had no connection with beyond the brief time we had spent together?

There was only one way to find out.

I closed my eyes and focused on my power centre. It immediately flared to life. My wings flexed at my back, and I spun the power within me, letting it grow into a powerful ball of healing energy. Then, with careful precision, I sent the power down through my arms and into my hands. Spin's throat was so small I was afraid I would tear it apart if I didn't temper the deluge of power, so I made it trickle through my fingers and into his flesh. In my mind's eye, I pictured the veins reconnecting, the muscles and tendons rejoining, the flesh mending. I could feel it all happening under my hands. When the last layer of his skin was whole again, I pulled my power back down my arms and collected it in my belly where it would wait for the next challenge.

I opened my eyes and looked at Spin. His face and throat were clean of blood, and I could see the perfectly healed skin of his throat, but he wasn't moving.

"Come on, Spin," I whispered. "Come on."

With a great heaving breath, Spin came to life. I helped him to his side, and he coughed up the blood and phlegm that had pooled in his throat. When he had finished hacking, he lay back against the stone and looked at me.

"Thank you, my lady." His voice was still weak, but his eyes held an internal strength.

"My pleasure."

"Now," he coughed and readjusted his position. "You must finish Big G."

"Agreed." We shared a grim smile.

I made sure Spin was as comfortable as possible and then dragged the dead minions up the passageway. As I dragged the two bodies, their blood streaming slowly behind them, I was disgusted with myself. This was the most violent thing I had ever done. It was beyond violent; it bordered on the sadistic. I was a healer, not a butcher, but the evil had taken over me. Regular me would have just knocked them out, evil me, well, evil me was not good. I tucked the bodies as best I could into a small alcove and returned to Spin. As I walked, I put my thoughts in order.

If evil was going to overtake me when things started getting violent, then I had to be ready for it. I had to use it to my advantage. I had to turn it against Greldrom and put an end to this horrible place. I checked on Spin one last time, putting the blade I had given him near his hand. Then I picked up my other blade and wiped it clean on my pants before re-sheathing it. I was already covered in minion blood, what was a bit more. I checked the positioning of my sword. It felt warm. The sword was ready for a fight, and so was I.

I squared my shoulders and slipped into the throne room.

45

I perched on the ledge high above the fray. No one noticed me; they were all too focused on their disgusting acts. I drew my sword. It flowed like silk from the sheath at my spine. I held it loosely at my side where it pulsed with its own white light. I took a deep breath and leapt from the ledge, my wings unfurling as I soared across the room.

A cry went up from the mass of minions below me. I locked eyes with Greldrom, and a smile played across his lips as I touched down before him. With a slight gesture of his hands, minions rushed in on me from all sides. I was expecting this and, using my wings as leverage, I spun in a low circle with my sword, slicing the first rush of minions across the belly. The next wave hesitated, and I used the moment to throw my energy out like a wave towards them. Fuelled by the darkness of the room, my energy moved with substantial force, knocking the minions back. They fell like dominoes, toppling over one another as they dropped to the floor of the chamber. My wave of power hit the stone walls of the chamber, and the entire space shook with the impact. All was silent as Greldrom spoke.

"No one move."

The few minions that had been trying to sneak out of the room stopped where they were.

"It appears we have a visitor."

I said nothing. I looked at my sword; it dripped with multicoloured blood. I swiped it through the air, blood flew freely from the blade, and soon it was gleaming again. A drop of bright pink landed on Greldrom's cheek.

"Is that any way to treat your host?" His voice gave away nothing as he gestured to the minion beside him.

With shaking hands and a bright white cloth, it wiped the smear of blood from Greldrom's face. I waited until the minion had retreated to its post before I spoke.

"I am here for your head."

A few of the younger minions gasped, others grunted their disbelief. Greldrom looked at me for a long moment, his face cold and hard, and then a gruesome smile crept across his face, and a deep, rolling laugh poured from his mouth. As he laughed the surrounding minions joined him. Tentatively at first and then more strongly. Soon the entire hall filled with the maniacal laughter of hundreds of minions. Greldrom sat at the centre of it all, his head thrown back, his blackened crooked teeth visible in the torchlight.

My sword was glowing more brightly at my side, and I could feel its power mingling with my own as a great loop of energy flowed between us. I glanced down at my hand and saw that it was glowing like the sword; I glanced again and realized the light was moving up my wrist. How long until I was entirely bathed in light, I thought to myself.

"Oh, Phoenix," Greldrom spoke above the laughter. "Thank you. I needed a good laugh." In the blink of an eye he regained his composure; his hands gripped the arms of his throne, the knuckles white with tension. "But you are trespassing in my home and this I cannot tolerate."

The laughter of the minions immediately stopped. In its absence the silence was deafening, a humming sound filled my ears as it pressed against me. The sword at my side twitched, and a soft light filled my peripheral vision, my entire arm now glowed.

"Your tyranny is over, Greldrom."

I felt power swell inside me. The glowing white light was now spreading across my chest. I saw Greldrom's eyes flick over my body and a glimmer of unease filled his eyes.

"Phoenix, I could kill you right now. I could have my many followers tear you to pieces right here. It would not take much, a mere flick of my wrist and they destroy you."

I raised a sceptical eyebrow, and the light spread down my other arm. Beneath my clothes, I felt it spread through my torso.

"Arrogance is an unattractive quality, Phoenix." Another raised eyebrow from me. "Do not mock me, bird!" His voice poured from him with rage. The power of it hit me hard, and I had to shift my feet and lean into it to stay upright. It roared like a wind and Greldrom shouted above the din. "I will not be disrespected in my own home!"

"No!" I shouted back, my power creating a shield before me, pushing against the wind of his rage. "You will die! And all those that stand between me and your death will die with you!"

"Ha!" Greldrom was now standing on his throne. Sweat beaded along his forehead and his hands were out in front of him as he attempted to fight me with his power. "You cannot defeat us all! You are alone here! A lone bird!" He bellowed into the room. "You will die alone!"

A high-pitched scream filled the air. Greldrom and I, both equally shocked by the sound, turned just as Archer entered the hall.

Archer came into the room like a hurricane. A colourful mess of minion blood covered his body, coating almost every inch of his chrome flesh. His hair was a mass of matted clumps, soaked as it was in the blood of minions. It hung in front of his face so I couldn't see his eyes as he swung his swords, one in each gore covered hand, almost faster than my eyes could track. He plowed into the room, cutting down minions like a farmer harvesting a field. The minions panicked. They ran from his blades, trampling each other. They fell back screaming, and a wave of frightened minions ran towards me as they tried desperately to get away from my lover's rage.

In my peripheral vision, I saw Greldrom leave his throne and run towards Archer. He had completely forgotten me as I stood so still in the room's turmoil. Time slowed to a trickle before me as I watched him move. I felt my power rise to a fever pitch inside me as every inch of my skin flared with white light. Slowly, ever so slowly, I raised my sword. My body moved as if through molasses. My wings pressed against the air, powering my torquing frame and outstretched sword. I saw my blade reach Greldrom's neck. It flared blue as it cut through his flesh. I saw the smoke rise in pale grey coils as it cauterized the wound. I watched calmly as the leader of the minions' head fell to the floor and rolled gently towards the throne.

46

———

The sound of minion screams filled my ears as suddenly everything returned to normal speed. Paying no attention to the chaos, I followed the path the skull had rolled. One of Greldrom's servants held the head in its tiny hands. It looked up at me, tears streaked its face.

"Thank you," it coughed, slurped. "Thank you."

"Give me the head," I whispered.

It held the head out to me. I sheathed my sword, taking a moment's pleasure as the steel slid like silk into its home. I then reached out and grasped the head by the ears. I gazed into the dead eyes. They were open wide, frozen in an expression of rage; the mouth stretched in a scream, a foul smell emanating from the gaping maw.

The minion beside me was speaking.

"Are you well, lady?"

"Hmm?"

I felt dazed. Power flowed up and down my spine in slow pulses. I couldn't believe it was done; it had been so easy.

Massive amounts of unspent adrenaline wandered through my veins.

"Are you well?"

"Am I well?" I asked the air. "Am I well…" A loud shout, a man's voice, tore through the air. "Archer!" I cried, snapping from my reverie.

I looked out across the room. Archer wasn't there, but I could hear him shouting up the passageway back to the surface, minions running after him. Evidently, they had overcome him and were now chasing him up the passage.

"No, please no," I said quietly, but the minion beside me heard my words.

"Stop!" he bellowed with unnatural volume. Every minion, even those at the mouth of the passage, stopped and turned to him. "Behold your new master! Do her bidding!" He gestured grandly at me, and every pair of eyes turned towards me. "Hold up the head, my lady," he said proudly.

I obeyed.

There was a moment of hushed hesitation and then every minion in the room, over a hundred sinewy bodies, dropped to their knees in supplication.

"Whoa," I murmured.

Apparently, I was the new leader of the minions. This was a situation too heavy to deal with immediately. First, I had to help Archer. I said to the group. "The others need to stop attacking, Archer."

"A moment, lady." The minion beside me seemed to have found his confidence and appointed himself my right-hand man. I watched as he closed his eyes and furrowed his brow for a moment, then he relaxed and looked at me. "It is done. The Archer has left the City of Caves."

"Shit!" I exclaimed and ran for the exit. I stopped after a

few steps, time to take advantage of my leadership position. I spread my wings and spoke to the group. "All those chained to walls must be freed and cared for." I pointed at Sid. He was still out cold. It made my heart hurt. "He, Sid, will be brought to the surface with me, and up there," I pointed to the break in the rock I had initially crawled through. "You will find the one you call, Spin. He is my friend, care for him and bring him to me at the surface."

"It will be done, my lady!" answered my right-hand man.

"What is your name?" I asked him. At first, he looked shocked but quickly recovered, a deep blush forming on his cheeks.

"Rogmesh, my lady."

"Thank you for your help, Rogmesh. I will see you at the surface."

He bowed deeply, then began ordering the other minions around. They had Sid quickly unchained, and a group of minions carried him behind me as I left the hall, Greldrom's skull still in my hands.

47

———

The journey to the surface was swift and uneventful. If you consider every minion I met bowing before me as I passed, uneventful. I was studiously ignoring the implications of their actions; I didn't want to be their new dictator. I had to find Archer and make sure he was okay, and then there was Sid to deal with. I hadn't taken a good look at him yet, but I had a feeling he would need some serious healing from me. At least I no longer had the Bounty to worry about. Word would spread quickly that Greldrom was dead and without him to provide a reward, the Void would surely stop hunting me. The fact that the minions now considered me their leader would also be a significant deterrent.

I could hear voices shouting. The sound was coming from outside the tunnel, and as I drew closer to the entrance, I could discern that one voice was Archer's.

The other was Mhyr's.

Shit.

And they were definitely fighting.

Double shit.

I broke into a jog, and the minions fell into line behind me. The quickened pace increased the sound of their footfalls. I glanced back to see all of them, literally all of them, following me up the passage.

"Crazy."

I could see the entrance up ahead. The sun had risen; it flooded the square before the entrance with light. After so long in the dark underground tunnels, my eyes streamed as they became accustomed to the brightness.

The two elite warriors were circling each other, getting close, but carefully not touching each other as they shouted. Even from the within the tunnel I could feel the tension between them. If they touched, terrible stuff would happen.

"How could you do such a thing?" Archer shouted.

"Me! You have betrayed your kind!" Mhyr screamed in his face.

"I will never love you! Never! You destroyed our love!" he shouted back.

"So you lay with her! A bird! You disgrace me with a bird!"

"Do not call her that!"

"You end our kind, you end true birth for a bird!" she spat back at him.

"You killed it, Mhyr. Your sick, twisted mind killed it." There was venom in Archer's voice.

"I am a warrior!" Mhyr sounded crazed. "That is who we are! She is weak! You have murdered our kind for a weak bird!"

"Weak?" I asked.

I stepped from the passage and into the light. My wings responded to the sun and stretched out to soak it in.

"You think me weak, Mhyr?" She was shaking, literally shaking with rage. "Does this look weak to you?"

I tossed the skull of Greldrom into the air. As it soared, the minions streamed out of the tunnel and formed a wide circle around the three of us. The head hit the ground at Mhyr's feet with a dull thud. Although her skin was the colour of buffed tin, she paled as she looked at the severed head of the former Lord of the Minions.

"Well done," Archer said proudly. His eyes were his own again. The evil of the caves no longer tugged at his soul.

"It cannot be," Mhyr whispered.

"Oh, it be, bitch," I countered. "It also be that you will get the hell out of here before I kick your ass." I sauntered towards her. "Greldrom is dead, the Bounty is over, there is nothing for you here."

Mhyr's eyes had not left Greldrom's cold orbs as I spoke, but she looked at me now. Her expression made me take a step back. She was smiling, a dark, twisted, crazy person smile.

"You truly are stupid, bird." She laughed; it sent shivers of ice up and down my spine. "You have helped me." She laughed again. "Yes, now I will not have to share your power with anyone."

"What?" My voice weakened as her words slowly made their way through my brain.

"What are you talking about, Mhyr?" Archer asked.

"Don't you see, Archer?" She laughed again and looked at me with such hatred it turned my stomach. "I am the one that set the Bounty."

48

Time had slowed when I beheaded Greldrom, but now it moved faster than my mind and heart could decipher. The word Bounty left the pewter mouth of Mhyr and Archer lunged at her. She was ready for it though, and in the blink of an eye she had torn a rib from her chest and thrown it at him. It hit Archer in the sternum; the force knocked him to the ground as the rib became black goo that spread over his chest, pinning him. As Archer fell, Mhyr tore more ribs from her chest and pirouetted, waving the bones in an arch through the air. As she did this, a film of silver energy flowed from the bones, trapping the two of us in an orb of power. It all happened so fast, inhumanly fast.

I was beyond outgunned.

"You sicken me, bird." Now that we were isolated, Mhyr's voice had become calm in a serial killer kind of way. "Always. Even before you were Banished, I hated you." She paced back and forth slowly, like a cat. "Yes, I knew that he wanted you even then. I knew you had caught his eye. So I set about engineering your undoing. I discovered your

Secrets. I planted the rumours. When you were finally Banished a great sense of relief filled me. I thought it was over. He would be mine again, and we could bring about the true birth our kind so sorely needed."

"True birth?" Even in mortal danger, I'm inquisitive. I need to work on that, if I get out of this alive.

"Stop playing dumb!" She screamed at me, and the force of it threw me against the silver orb. I bounced off the side and hit the ground, my skin tingling where it had contacted the silvery substance.

"Damn it, Mhyr!" The shock was wearing off, and anger was seeping in. "I really don't know! I've got no memory of the Void!"

"Oh, that's right, I'm sorry." She was serial killer calm again. "Most Travellers just appear, fully formed, amongst their kind. A true birth is very rare, very, very rare." She shook her head slowly with each 'very.' It was very, very creepy. "It is much like a mortal birth. Two Travellers of opposite genders, a rarity itself, must meet and bond. They then mate and breed and the true birth occurs."

"Okay, so just like a mortal birth," I said from the ground, my legs were too weak for me to stand.

"I do not know the base acts of humans," Myhr said with a wave of her hand.

"So you're angry with me because Archer won't have sex with you?"

"No!" She was on me in a second, grabbing me by the neck and dragging me to my feet. "I am angry because he stopped being my mate! I am angry because after he laid eyes on you, he no longer wanted me! I am angry," she was screaming in my face, her spit spraying me. "Because you killed my true birth! You destroyed my chance at life!" She punched me in the gut so hard I vomited. My puke sprayed her chest, but she paid no attention to it. "And now I will destroy yours!"

With immense physical strength, she flipped me around, breaking the fine bones of my wings as she pressed my back to her chest and wrapped her arm around my throat. My wings were mashed against her, broken and useless. I tried with all my strength to pull her arm from my throat, but with her free hand she punched me in the back of the head, stunning me.

From this position, I could now see what was happening outside Mhyr's orb. Archer was still on the ground, fighting valiantly against the black ooze that was bent on keeping him pinned to the ground. The minions were taking turns throwing themselves at the orb itself. Over and over they threw themselves at the silver energy, singeing their flesh, crying out in pain and rage as they tried to save me.

"I will have your power," Mhyr was whispering in my ear. In my helpless state, her energy invaded my body, looking for my core, seeking the deepest part of me. "And after I have your power, I will eat your wings." She licked my earlobe. "I bet they are delicious."

It was too much, her words in my ear, Archer struggling before me, the minions running and screaming everywhere. It felt like my Banishment all over again, the memory of it brought an overwhelming wave of terror to my body. At first, it was cold, ice cold, and then somewhere in the vortex of pain and fear it changed. The ice in me began to melt. Through the fear, I could glimpse fire.

Mhyr's hot breath was on my neck, her arm around my throat tightened. Breathing was becoming more and more difficult. Mhyr was chanting something, a stream of words too quiet and mumbled for me to hear. As she chanted, the tendrils of her power dug into me more deeply. They wrapped around my heart and started to squeeze. That is when I screamed.

"Good!" Mhyr broke her chant to shout over me. "That means it's working, bird! Soon you will be mine!"

The squeezing was getting tighter, my vision was going black. The minions pounded on the orb, Archer struggled on the ground. A small part of me could hear him yelling my name, and the heat in me grew. I was so warm now; I felt as if I was cooking from the inside out, my skin felt like it would blister.

"What are you doing?" Mhyr asked, her voice angry and yet unsure.

I thought it was Mhyr's power that was making me burn, but I was wrong. This was coming from inside me. I couldn't speak around her choke hold. She shook me hard and screamed the question again.

"What are you doing?"

I grabbed at her arm; it did nothing to stop her, but when I looked down at my hands, I saw that my skin had erupted in angry red blisters. I strained my eyes to take in my arms. They were also covered in large fluid filled boils. Mhyr grunted in my ear as her hold on my heart tightened.

"I don't know what you're doing, but we will end this now."

The pain was immense. I felt the blisters on my arms burst. Hot fluid covered my face and dripped down my arms. Mhyr was screaming but refused to let me go. The heat within me doubled, burning my very soul. Flames sprang up from hands. They moved like quicksilver, engulfing my arms, torso and legs. My vision filled with orange light as my face and hair became a flaming mass. Finally, my broken wings burst into blinding white fiery flames.

Mhyr let go of me.

But I was too far gone. I barely felt her power retreat. I just burned. I stood there and looked down at my flaming body. I was a pillar of fire. I felt the orb dissolve. I felt my many minions fall on Mhyr like a wave of angry flesh. I saw Archer stand before me, tears streaming down his face as he screamed my name.

And still I burned.

I burned and watched the flesh peel from my hands. I burned until I saw bone in my outstretched wings. I burned and burned. And when I thought I could stand no more, everything went black.

49

———

I was lying on a very firm surface. White light was forcing its way through my eyelids. I opened my eyes to find myself in a room of pure white stone. I could feel a light breeze, and a glance to my left showed me a large open window through which I could see blue sky. I tried to move my head, but my neck was very stiff. The room was empty save for the bed I lay on, a simple wooden chair beside it and a mirror. It was large and rested against the wall at an angle that prevented me from looking into the glass from where I lay.

I was covered in a pure white sheet. I could see the outline of my feet and body, but I was smaller than I remembered. With a shock, I realised I could not feel the sheet against my skin. I felt nothing. I only felt the bed because gravity pulled me against it. I felt the breeze because it pressed against my face.

"Where am I?" My voice sounded like a dry reed.

"Good. You're awake."

If I could have moved, I would have. The sound of the

man's voice and his sudden appearance in the once empty chair scared the crap out of me.

"What the hell!" I exclaimed from my frozen position on the bed.

"You're all right, calm down."

"Calm down?!"

He was old; he looked about seventy, but in the Void, he could have been a thousand. He was slim and wiry, with bony limbs and long grey hair that hung limply around his face.

He also had wings.

Just like mine.

"Who are you?" I asked, trying to stay calm. He had wings. He had wings just like mine!

"I am a friend." He smiled, his bristled chin twitching like it hadn't been used for the purpose in a long while.

"What's your name?"

"Royal."

"Okay, Royal, are you like me?"

"Not really." He laughed, it was a warm sound. "But if you mean species, are we the same species, then yes. I am like you."

"Really?" I could feel tears starting to trickle down my face.

"Really." He looked at me kindly and pulled his chair closer to the head of the bed. "I heard your call and came running, girl. You are not alone. We have each other now."

He placed his hand gently on the sheet where the bump of my hand was.

"Are you my dad?" I choked the word out over my tears.

"No, girl. You are not a true birth."

True birth. Mhyr. Archer. Minions.

"Archer! The minions! What happened to them?" I struggled to sit up, Royal placed a gentle hand on my shoulder and held me down.

"Easy girl, you've had quite the shock. You need to take things slowly."

"What happened, Royal, what happened after I burned?"

"When I got to you they were gone." I half screamed, half sobbed at his words, and he rushed to calm me. "But that doesn't mean they're hurt. When you burned up your power would have blown across that clearing and scattered them to the four winds. I'm sure they're fine, and when you're healthy, you can go and find them."

"Archer?" My heart hurt so much.

"Archer? The silver fella on the Guard?" He looked at me kindly. "Darling, no one but our kind could have approached your flame. Even if he'd wanted to, he wouldn't have been able to withstand the blast when you finally blew."

"So you brought me here?"

"I brought you here."

"When can I see him again?"

"You might want to wait until you've healed," Royal looked conflicted as he continued. "You don't look so pretty."

"He won't care," I said proudly. Royal patted my arm, and I realised I was itchy. Very itchy.

"Why am I so itchy?" I moved my arm to scratch the other, and like lightning, Royal's hand was there to stop me.

"Don't scratch."

"But why am I itchy everywhere?" I tried to wriggle from his grasp.

"Try to stay calm." Royal held me down.

"You stay calm!" I shouted. "I think I'll freak out, thank you!"

I pushed against him again, and he let me go. I threw back the sheet and sprung from the bed. Every inch of me hurt as I did it, like my skin was a piece of ice being cracked by a hammer.

I was now in full view of the mirror.

I wanted to scream. I wanted to dissolve into a puddle of tears. I wanted to weep and rage at what I saw, but I stayed silent. The image in the glass was the worst thing I'd ever seen and my mind shut down around it.

I was a stretched frame of raw meat and bone, a mass of red and black. All the flesh had melted from my body, leaving only sinew and skeleton behind. My breasts were gone, melted away, and there were gaps between my ribs that weren't completely covered by the dry tendon that stretched over my matchstick frame. I could see the shadow of my lungs working within their cage. My arms were bones wrapped in red ribbon, the crest of my pelvis was white where it poked through the last layer of fascia that stuck to the bone. My hair was gone. My lips were strips of rough leather. I blinked and watched my eyelids barely close over my blue eyes. And my wings, my beautiful wings. Gone. The vibrant colours that used to frame me had been obliterated, and now only bones remained. Bits of meat were stuck to them like a carcass not quite picked clean.

"Breathe, Phoenix, breathe," Royal's voice was soothing, and my lungs heaved to life at its coaxing. "This happens to us all."

He rose from his chair, pulling the sheet from the bed as he moved. He turned me from the glass and wrapped me in the clean white sheet, tucking away the horror of my body. I wept, and he held me gently, careful not to put too much pressure on my frame as his wings engulfed us.

He whispered in my ear.

"You will heal."
I choked through my sobs.
"I damn well better."

THE END

CONTINUE THE ADVENTURE...
Mend the Flesh
The Phoenix Series Book 3
Available Now

THE STORY DOESN'T END HERE

The story doesn't end here.

If this book stirred something in you—

if you want more of the strange, the cinematic, or the stories that meet you where the shadows are deepest—

you're in the right place.

When you sign up for my mailing list, you'll get early access to new releases, behind-the-scenes lore, letters from my strange and unusual world, and first word when new episodes of my podcast *We Make Art* go live.

Sign up and join me on this adventure:
https://sarahrockwood.com/mailing-list/

SPREAD THE WORD

If this book moved you, let it move others too.

Reviews are powerful. They help stories like this find their way into the right hands—and into the quiet hearts that need them most.

If you enjoyed what you just read, consider leaving a review on your favourite book-loving platform and the store where you picked it up. Even a few words can make a difference.

And if it stirred something worth sharing, tell your people. Whisper it, post it, pass it on.

You're part of how this story travels.

Thank you.

MEND THE FLESH

"Where are my blades?"

Royal was sitting on a low stool in the yellow sand of his desert hideaway. He rose stiffly to his feet.

"Why are you out of bed, girl?"

"Don't call me 'girl,' it's demeaning," I approached him. "Where are my blades?"

Royal let out a sound of acquiescence.

"I put it somewhere safe."

We were standing almost toe to toe now, like two bedraggled vultures who were both picked clean. Royal metaphorically and me physically. Okay, and emotionally.

"You don't look so good, honey. You need to get back inside. The sun will tear you up with you so raw."

"Take me to my blades."

"Blade. I found one blade," he grunted. "And it's inside, so you might as well head back in there."

I turned on my bony heel and shuffled back into the adobe dwelling. It had been two full days since I'd awoken in this home, raw and burnt down to the bone. How am I still alive, you ask? Well, apparently this what my people do.

Every once in a while if we get very, very stressed we burst into flames. Our wings, our flesh, everything, burning down to bone and sinew, culminating in a giant blast of power. And God help whoever is standing close by.

I don't know what happened to those people. I was locked in a battle for my life when I burned. Mhyr, my boyfriend's crazy ex, had an arm wrapped around my throat and was trying to drain me of my power. Archer, my boyfriend, Mhyr's ex, you get the idea, and about three hundred minions were trying to save me. Unfortunately, Mhyr had surrounded us with an impenetrable dome of power so they couldn't get in. As Mhyr had pulled on my power, my body had freaked out and this ability to regenerate, burst into flames, that I hadn't known about, took over. It scared the crap out of me. I was sure I would die. Archer was sure, too. I could see him on the other side of the dome screaming my name, tears running down his face. So I had burst into flames and woken up here, alone.

Well, not alone, Royal was here. Royal, another of my kind, not my father, even though he sure tried to act like it, was at my bedside. When I had finally given into the burning, and my power had blasted the dome free and shot out across the land, Royal heard my call. I thought I was the only one of our kind, so you can imagine my surprise when I woke up to a grizzled old man with big multi-coloured wings staring down at me. Picture Kris Kristofferson dressed as an angel for Halloween, that's Royal.

"Where is it?" I demanded.

We were now inside, though in this case inside was a relative term. There were no doors in the doorways or glass in the windows; Royal's home was an adobe hut comprising arched ceiling rooms that connected to each other by breezy passages. Despite the heat of the sun outside, inside was cool and shady. Night got cold though, so the primary rooms and sleeping areas had fire pits.

"I put it in the kitchen," he said mildly as he crossed to the cooking area, his fading wings dragging ever so slightly on the floor. "Seemed the best place for something that sharp." On the kitchen counter was my untouched bowl of porridge. Royal glanced at it. "You need to eat."

"I'm not hungry."

"Yes, you are." He bent down to open a cabinet while he talked. "But it hurts your gut; I get it. But if you don't eat, you won't regenerate. And if you don't regenerate, you can't go home to whoever gave you this."

He placed the blade next to my cold porridge.

It was the short sword Archer had given me long before my Banishment, the beautiful blade that had called to me in my weapons room in what seemed like a lifetime ago. I stepped up to the counter and moved to touch the hilt, then hesitated. My raw, sinewy fingers held inches above it. I was sure that if I touched the blade, it would call to Archer. Archer. He was probably losing his mind looking for me. Or he assumed I was dead. And right now he'd be right. Sort of. I looked dead. I looked like I had been rotting in a coffin for months and then changed my mind and started walking around again. I was literally bone, sinew and the odd bit of flesh. I had no hair, no lips, half an eyelid on one eye and, although a thin layer of tissue had grown over my chest cavity, in the light you could see my lungs.

I looked like a walking horror movie. I didn't want Archer to see me like this. I didn't want anyone to see me like this. I tolerated Royal's eyes on me because he'd been through this before and as much as it pissed me off; I needed help. My arms were too stiff to wrap myself up in the light sheets I wore; Royal did that. He also cleaned the last of the dead burnt flesh off my exposed spine and changed the damp sponge I'd had to wear over my eyes those first few days. I couldn't get better without him. I gingerly sat on a stool and began eating my cold porridge.

"Please put that away," I swallowed. It hurt. I got another spoonful. "Thank you. For everything." A tear rolled from my naked eyeball, the salt stung as it travelled down my cheek.

"It's my pleasure," Royal mumbled. Then he picked up the sword. "I'll put this in your room." As he walked past, he placed a hand ever so lightly on my shoulder. "You'll get better real soon, honey." And then he left me to my porridge.

- 2 -

The days are long in the desert; especially when you have no books or music or television. It doesn't seem to bother Travellers, but I grew up in the human world, and in the human world there's a lot of good tv. I tried talking to Royal, but he preferred to spend the day outside sunning himself on a rock, only coming in occasionally to cook me some porridge or go to the bathroom. The only time we spent together was at night.

After dinner, when the sun was down, he would build fires in all the rooms and then we'd sit together in the living room. Him deep in a beanbag chair and me sitting painfully upright on a straight-back chair that provided enough support for the skeletal remains on my wings. Tonight was the third night of this routine and I longed for conversation as I watched Royal stare at the flames.

"Any adventures you'd like to share?" I asked.

"Hmm?"

"Adventures. You must have a few," I pressed.

"Not really."

"Right." This was going well. "Any bird-person wisdom you'd like to impart to me?"

He turned from the flame and looked at me, the light blue of his eyes seemed to spark in the light.

"Bird-people? Is that what you think we are?"

There was an edge to his voice that I hadn't heard before. I'd struck a nerve. Which was fine with me because sitting here in silence was making me crazy. If having an argument with him was the only way to get him to talk, then so be it.

"I don't know what we are. Until a few days ago, I thought I was the only bird-person around. I meet you and think 'fantastic, now I can learn who we are,' but you don't seem to want to tell me. So until I know different, I'm going with bird-people."

"Bird is their word. Not ours."

"Who are 'they?'"

"Everyone else."

"Okay." Ah, that familiar Traveller crypticness, how I'd missed you. "So what's our word?"

"I'm Royal, and you're Phoenix. And that's all we need."

"So we don't have a name for our species like the Sirens or the Minions do?"

"Nope, don't need one."

"Why not?"

"Because until a few days ago, honey, I was sure I was the only one of whatever we are. And I was fine with Royal."

"Really? You've never met another of our kind?"

"Nope."

"Then..." I paused, "then how did you know to come help me?"

Royal sighed heavily and with a few flaps of his wings

was standing. He moved towards the fire and added another log. I stayed silent, waiting.

"Well, because that explosion of power you let off, and the scream that came with it, they felt just like it did when it happened to me. I'm sitting outside on my rock and suddenly this ripping scream goes through me and every feather in my wings stands on end. I got this image of you, this burnt out thing lying in the dirt, and my heart knew where you were and what had happened to you. So I Travelled to you. Brought you back here." He turned to me, a rough smile on his lips. "Don't go thanking me again. You've done enough of that." He went back to his seat. "And I know you'd do the same thing for me."

"I would."

"I know, honey, you're good people. Good bird-people," he winked.

"Oh, please don't make me laugh." I tried to relax into the shaking of my ribs. "It hurts."

"You're getting better though, more meat on you today."

"Yeah, a bit."

We sat in companionable silence for a few minutes.

"So how many times has this," I gestured at myself, "happened to you?"

"Twice."

"Seriously?" If I'd had eyebrows or even eyelids, they would have shot up. "You've been through this twice?"

"Yep, a long time ago now."

"How did it happen?"

"Well, the first time was sticky."

I waited in the firelight. How many times had I sat round a fire with a fellow Traveller and learned their secrets? Sid had told me my life story by a fire like this. I heard about the capture me so he could claim the reward. I didn't feel bad about killing him. I'd thought long and hard about it those first few days I laid on my bed here in Royal's home. Greldrom needed to die. So I killed him. I could live with that and still sleep at night. Which honestly scared me more than the actual killing.

Even though I wasn't human, I still wanted to keep my humanity.

"Right, I just thought when we were outside our world we were safe."

"Phoenix, you've got a lot more to learn."

"I know," I looked down at my sinewy fingers; they looked like shrivelled pepperoni in the firelight. I shuddered, sliding my hands into the folds of my robes. "Sorry, I'll stop interrupting. You were gliding over the mountains?"

Royal had watched my brief finger moment but said nothing. Then with a great shuddering sigh he began his tale.

Mend The Flesh is available now from your favourite retailer!

ABOUT THE AUTHOR

Sarah Rockwood is a storyteller of the strange and unusual. Her fiction reads like film—visceral, lyrical, and a little bit odd. Tales that invite readers into shadowed worlds where heroines reclaim their power one scene at a time. Her writing and music have appeared in film, television, and bookshelves across the globe.

Raised on a steady diet of *The Muppets*, *David Bowie*, and *The Rocky Horror Picture Show*, her stories are likely to keep you turning pages well past your bedtime.

For more of the strange and unusual, visit:

SarahRockwood.com